Bloody Autumn

THE SHENANDOAH VALLEY CAMPAIGN
OF 1864

By Daniel T. Davis
and Phillip S. Greenwalt

EMERGING CIVIL WAR SERIES

Chris Mackowski, *series editor*
Cecily Nelson Zander, *chief historian*

The Emerging Civil War Series

offers compelling, easy-to-read overviews of some of the Civil War's most important battles and issues.

Recipient of the Army Historical Foundation's Lieutenant General Richard G. Trefry Award for contributions to the literature on the history of the U.S. Army

Other titles in the Emerging Civil War Series include:

All the Fighting They Want: The Atlanta Campaign from Peachtree Creek to the City's Surrender, July 18-September 2, 1864 by Stephen Davis

Calamity in Carolina: The Battles of Averasboro and Bentonville, March 1865 by Daniel T. Davis and Phillip S. Greenwalt

Call Out the Cadets: The Battle of New Market, May 15, 1864 by Sarah Kay Bierle

The Carnage was Fearful: The Battle of Cedar Mountain, August 9, 1862 by Michael Block

Grant's Left Hook: The Bermuda Hundred Campaign, May 5-June 7, 1864 by Sean Michael Chick

Hurricane from the Heavens: The Battle of Cold Harbor, May 26-June 5, 1864 by Daniel T. Davis and Phillip S. Greenwalt

John Brown's Raid: Harpers Ferry and the Coming of the Civil War, October 16-18, 1859 by Jon-Erik Gilot and Kevin Pawlak

Let Us Die Like Men: The Battle of Franklin, Nov. 30, 1864 by William Lee White

A Long and Bloody Task: The Atlanta Campaign from Dalton through Kennessaw to the Chat-tahoochee, May 5-July 18, 1864 by Stephen Davis

The Most Desperate Acts of Gallantry: George A. Custer in the Civil War by Daniel T. Davis

Out Flew the Sabres: The Battle of Brandy Station, June 9, 1863 by Eric J. Wittenberg and Daniel T. Davis

For a complete list of titles in the Emerging Civil War Series, visit www.emergingcivilwar.com

Bloody Autumn

THE SHENANDOAH VALLEY CAMPAIGN OF 1864

By Daniel T. Davis
and Phillip S. Greenwalt

EMERGING CIVIL WAR SERIES

SB

Savas Beatie

California

ISBN-13: 978-1-61121-165-8

Library of Congress Control Number: 2013954086

Third edition, first printing 2023

Published by
Savas Beatie LLC
989 Governor Drive, Suite 102
El Dorado Hills, California 95762
Phone: 916-941-6896
Email: sales@savasbeatie.com
Web: www.savasbeatie.com

Savas Beatie titles are available at special discounts for bulk purchases in the United States by corporations, institutions, and other organizations. For more details, please contact Special Sales, P.O. Box 4527, El Dorado Hills, CA 95762, or you may e-mail us as at sales@savasbeatie.com, or visit our website at www.savasbeatie.com for additional information.

Daniel:
To Willie Chapel Pettus, III
December 28, 1973, to September 23, 2009
We miss you, brother . . . .

Phillip:
To my parents, Stephen and Melanie, who inspired my love of history.

Table of Contents

List of Maps

Maps by Hal Jespersen

Acknowledgments

Both authors would like to express their joint sincerity and gratitude to the following people who have, like the soldiers who fought, given their all to help us in the publication of this book.

To the great historians at Emerging Civil War, especially Chris Mackowski and Kristopher D. White, who sent the pitch to Savas Beatie, organized the ECW series, and proofread through multiple drafts: we greatly appreciate everything you both have done and continue to do. Thank you.

A footbridge leads to the American Battlefield Trust property at Fisher's Hill. (cm)

To Theodore Savas and the Savas Beatie team who took the chance on us: we hope we have reflected that trust well and look forward to continued work with you.

To Hal Jespersen, whose excellent maps really enhance the flow of the story: we thank you, Hal, for your patience and commitment, even when we threw some challenges of driving tour maps at you!

To the renowned historian on the Shenandoah Valley campaign of 1864, Scott Patchan. He graciously wrote an excellent introduction for the book.

Besides the great historians at ECW who helped us in this endeavor, we would like to extend another hearty thanks to the staff and volunteers at Cedar Creek and Belle Grove National Historical Park, especially Chief of Interpretation Eric Campbell, who graciously consented to writing a great appendix for us. In addition, Park Rangers Shannon Moeck and Kyle Rothemich both showed the level of enthusiasm and service that reflects the high standard one comes to expect from rangers of the National Park Service. They were both there to assist in any way they could, from driving us to the 8th Vermont Monument to searching through files to see the extent of Gen. Cullen Battle's leg wound. Park Volunteer Patrick Kehoe, a member of the Cedar Creek Battlefield Association, asked some poignant questions that directed and focused our attention and opened up great historical conversations while showing his deep interest in the Valley. To Heather Ball for accompanying us on trips to Fisher's Hill and cemeteries and the pictures she took along the way, thank you. We could not forget Joe Ball, either.

Prior to being co-authors, we were each shaped in our growth as historians by the following people.

Daniel: My lovely wife Katy for all of her love, patience, and support. You are the great blessing in my life. I love you more each day. To my parents, Tommy and Kathy Davis. At a very young age, through many family vacations and weekend trips, they instilled a deep respect and love of American history and the Civil War. My brother Matt also accompanied my father and me on a trip to take pictures at Fisher's Hill, Tom's Brook, and Cedar Creek. To my aunt and uncle, Butch and Margie Markham, who continued the battlefield excursions through my college years. To the renowned historian Frank O'Reilly, who first showed me Fisher's Hill and Cedar Creek so many years ago. Lastly, to my wife's parents, Tom and Cathy Bowen. I began this project living in their house while my wife and I worked to build our own. I am forever in their debt.

Phillip: To my parents, Stephen and Melanie, as the dedication reads, for their nurturing, inspiration, love, and support. I know everyone says this, but they are truly the greatest parents. I have always looked forward to escaping to battlefields with my father. To my sister and brother, Adrienne and Patrick: thanks for the laughs, support, and putting up with me as I tried to tell you in conversation "how cool" this one account I found from a soldier was. To all my extended family—this includes many history enthusiasts—thank you also for the great conversations and love over the years. Lastly, to the staff at George Washington Birthplace National Monument and Thomas Stone National Historic Site, a great bunch of historians.

PHOTO CREDITS: Historical photographs courtesy of Fredericksburg and Spotsylvania National Military Park (fsnmp); the Library of Congress (loc); Museum of the Confederacy (moc); Son of the South (sos); Virginia Military Institute (vmi); and Western Reserve Historical Society (wrhs). Modern photography courtesy of the authors, Dan Davis and Phill Greenwalt (dd/pg), Heather Ball (hb), and Chris Mackowski (cm).

The Mainers have a monument at Third Winchester. (pg)

For the Emerging Civil War Series

Theodore P. Savas, *publisher*
Chris Mackowski, *series editor*
Cecily Nelson Zander, *chief historian*
Sarah Keeney, *editorial consultant*
Veronica Kane, *production supervisor*   Maps by Hal Jespersen
Kristopher D. White, *co-founding editor*   Design and layout by Chris Mackowski

Foreword

BY SCOTT PATCHAN

The 1864 Shenandoah Valley campaign resulted from the determined campaign of Gen. U. S. Grant and his hammering style of conducting simultaneous offensives across the so-called Southern Confederacy. When he first took command of all United States forces in early 1864, Grant readily recognized that the Shenandoah Valley had been a constant nuisance to Union commanders since the war began. In 1861, a failed Union offensive there allowed Gen. Joseph E. Johnston and an obscure brigadier from Lexington, Virginia, named Thomas J. Jackson to leave the Valley and play the decisive role in the Confederate victory at the battle of Bull Run. In 1862, Jackson's marches and maneuvers in the Valley befuddled several Union commanders and led to Federal defeat. More importantly, those setbacks in the Valley prompted President Abraham Lincoln to fear for the safety of Washington, D.C., and withhold vital reinforcements from Maj. Gen. George B. McClellan as his Army of the Potomac inched ever closer to Richmond. In 1863, Lt. Gen. Richard S. Ewell's thrashing of the hapless Maj. Gen. Robert Milroy's forces at the second battle of Winchester opened the door for Gen. Robert E. Lee's second invasion of the north, which culminated in the epic battle of Gettysburg.

Grant set about to change that in the spring of 1864, but a combination of inept Federal leadership and Confederate aggressiveness stymied his designs. Politics dictated that Grant place German Maj. Gen. Franz Sigel in command of the forces operating in the Valley, although he was a known bungler. His

The Virginia Military Institute's Hall of Valor, including the Virginia Museum of the Civil War, overlooks the 300-acre New Market battlefield. In May of 1864, cadets from VMI rushed to the aid of Confederate forces commanded by Maj. Gen. John C. Breckenridge to repulse an incursion by Union Maj. Gen. Franz Sigel. The battle was the latest in an ongoing string of encounters in the Valley that eventually led to a major effort by Federals to sweep it clean in the late summer and fall of 1864. (cm)

sluggish campaign and piecemeal tactics allowed the former vice president of the United States and then Maj. Gen. John C. Breckinridge to assemble a force from far flung regions of Southwestern Virginia and West Virginia in time to rout Sigel at New Market on May 15. Breckinridge then took his troops east and played a part in defeating Grant at the battle of Cold Harbor.

Typically, Grant did not give up but replaced Sigel with the more capable Maj. Gen. David Hunter six days after New Market. Hunter rejuvenated and reorganized the Union forces in the Valley and renewed the offensive. With Breckinridge gone, Lee ordered Brig. Gen. William E. "Grumble" Jones to bring nearly 6,000 men from Southwestern Virginia and East Tennessee to confront Hunter's advance. The two sides met in the shadows of the Blue Ridge in eastern Augusta County on June 5 near the tiny village of Piedmont. In a battle that saw more men killed and wounded than any battle previously fought in the Shenandoah Valley, Hunter routed the Confederate forces and occupied Staunton the next day. Reinforced by Maj. Gen. George Crook's forces from West Virginia, Hunter then moved against Lynchburg, a vital Confederate logistical center. Lee could not risk its loss and sent Lt. Gen. Jubal A. Early to save it from destruction. Early easily succeeded in driving the tentative Hunter back into the mountains of West Virginia and then launched his own offensive down the Shenandoah Valley. He crossed the Potomac River, defeated a small Federal force at the battle of Monocacy on July 9, and marched to the outskirts of Washington by the afternoon on July 11. Learning that two Federal army corps were on the way to the Federal capital, Early cancelled plans for an all-out attack the next morning and instead marched away under cover of darkness, ultimately returning to the Shenandoah Valley.

By July 24, Early was back on the offensive in the Valley seeking to carry out Robert E. Lee's objective of diverting Union troops to the Valley from the Richmond and Petersburg front. Early attacked George Crook at the second battle of Kernstown, routing him back into Maryland and clearing the way for Jubal's second raid north of the Potomac River. This time, Early sent his cavalry on a punitive raid into Pennsylvania, burning Chambersburg, Pennsylvania, to the ground.   Although Gen.

Scott C. Patchan serves as a director on the board of the Kernstown Battlefield Association in Winchester, Virginia, and is a member of the Shenandoah Valley Battlefield Foundation's Resource Protection Committee. He is the author of many articles and books, including Shenandoah Summer: The 1864 Valley Campaign (2007) and The Last Battle of Winchester: Phil Sheridan, Jubal Early, and the Shenandoah Valley Campaign (2013).

William W. Averell tracked down the raiders and wrecked their force at the battle of Moorefield, West Virginia, the damage had been done.

Early's actions belied the message that Abraham Lincoln was trumpeting in his campaign to be reelected president of the United States in 1864. Lincoln urged the Northern electorate to "stay the course" as Union forces were heading toward ultimate victory. Early's appearance at the gates of Washington and the burning of Chambersburg belied Lincoln's claims and left open the very real possibility of a peace candidate defeating the president and opening the door to a negotiated settlement that saw the breakup of the Union and the restoration of slavery in the South.

Grant readily recognized the political realities that resulted from the military actions within and emanating from the Shenandoah Valley and took prompt remedial action. The Sixth and Nineteenth Army Corps returned to the Valley, and Grant sent Maj. Gen. Philip H. Sheridan to take command. What ensued was the largest, bloodiest, and most consequential series of events that occurred in the Shenandoah Valley during the course of the war.

In the ensuing text, Dan and Phill provide both veteran and novice students of the Civil War with a well-written summary of the campaign between Sheridan and Early that culminated with the former winning a series of four major victories in a 30 day period and that also witnessed the destruction of the Shenandoah Valley's mills and agricultural assets, an act that crippled its ability to support Confederate operations within its bounds. Dan and Phill weave an excellent summary of the campaign that will serve to introduce those new to the Civil War to the events of that "Bloody Autumn" and will serve as a ready refresher for veteran stompers who are heading out to visit those storied fields of conflict.

Scott C. Patchan

"In pushing up the Shenandoah Valley . . .

it is desirable that nothing should be left

to invite the enemy to return. Take all provisions,

forage, and stock wanted for the use of your command;

such as cannot be consumed, destroy."

— *Lt. Gen. Ulysses S. Grant*
to Maj. Gen. Philip Sheridan

Prologue

The message raced along the Shenandoah Valley via signal flag and reached the Confederate Army of the Valley on the night of October 16, 1864. Major General Stephen Dodson Ramseur, in charge of one of the three infantry divisions in Lt. Gen. Jubal Early's army, was the recipient of joyous news: Ellen "Nellie" Richmond Ramseur, his wife, had given birth.

"His joy was full deep in his heart," an observer later wrote in a letter to Nellie. Ramseur had "tears of sympathy for you."

Ramseur hailed from North Carolina, where he was born on May 31, 1837. He attended Davidson College for a year at the age of 16 but left to accept an appointment to the United States Military Academy at West Point in 1855. Graduating from the academy on the brink of hostilities in 1860, he resigned on April 6, 1861. His first command with the Confederacy was as a captain in the artillery, and he saw service on the Virginia Peninsula under Maj. Gen. John Bankhead Magruder. In April 1862, Ramseur was elected colonel of the 49th North Carolina Infantry and led the regiment through the Seven Day's campaign, where he received his first of many wounds when a musket ball broke his right arm above the elbow. He would suffer from paralysis of the arm and recuperated between Richmond and his family home in Lincolnton, North Carolina.

Ramseur earned his promotion to brigadier general through this ordeal on November 1, 1862. He took over the brigade formerly commanded by George B. Anderson, a fellow North Carolinian who was mortally wounded at the battle of Antietam. Ramseur's first major action in command of the brigade was at Chancellorsville, where he was wounded again when a shell fragment struck him in the leg. He was transported back to Richmond and

Stephen Ramseur lays at rest in the St. Luke Episcopal Church Cemtery in Lincolnton, North Carolina. (hb)

Maj. Gen. Stephen Dodson Ramseur (fsnmp)

treated there. Ramseur was supposedly so incapacitated that a lady friend he dined with had to cut his food for him. However, the strong-willed Tar Heel was back in command of the brigade for the Gettysburg campaign.

After active campaigning ended in the middle of October 1863, Ramseur rushed home. He had pushed back his wedding to Nellie from mid-September; on October 28, they finally married at Woodside plantation in Milton, North Carolina—Nellie's birthplace.

By the spring of 1864, Ramseur was a rising star in the Army of Northern Virginia. After surviving the first battle of the Overland campaign in the Wilderness, Ramseur again attracted the attention of a Union musket. At the battle of Spotsylvania Court House, a minie ball stuck him in the right arm, completely passing through the limb slightly below the elbow. Ramseur refused to leave the field.

He regained his strength and, by the end of May, was appointed to command Jubal Early's old division. The redoubtable Ramseur was up to the task and, the following month, was promoted to major general.

Ramseur would serve that summer in all the Second Corps' engagements, from Lynchburg to Maryland. Back in Virginia, he fought through battles against Union Gen. Philip Sheridan's forces. The latest in that string of maneuvers had brought the Confederate army to Fisher's Hill, where Ramseur was in camp when the cheerful news of fatherhood finally arrived on that October 17 morning.

After his initial elation subsided, Ramseur composed himself to write a letter to his beloved Nellie. He wanted to know all the details, from the sex of the baby, to how Nellie was feeling. He also made an attempt to relay the love he felt for his wife and child. The overjoyed new father and husband expressed that he could not love his wife more than he did at that very instant, loving her "more devotedly, tenderly than ever before." He thanked and marveled at how God had brought her safely through labor and the mercy He had shown both of them during this time. Ramseur would write of the future, "may He soon reunite us in happiness & peace a joyful family," he concluded.

Ramseur would never be reunited with his family, though, nor know the sex of his child.

Forgotten in that brief interlude of familial joy was the war, which came intruding back the following day. Ramseur was called to Early's headquarters to be briefed on future operations. Doubtlessly feeling his new responsibility, Ramseur composed a will before leaving for the meeting with Early and the other officers.

The meeting would culminate in the battle of Cedar Creek, fought on October 19, 1864. During the battle, late in the afternoon, Ramseur was mortally wounded

when a bullet entered his right side, passed through both lungs, and finally lodged below his left arm.

Grimes, who had sat and shared with Ramseur the great news of him being a father, wrote two weeks after the battle about the "death of the brave and heroic soldier." The fellow Tar Heel said the loss of Ramseur was "not only a loss to this division but to his State and the country at large. No truer or nobler spirit has been sacrificed."

The Confederacy's autumn campaign in the Shenandoah Valley suffered a mortal wound at Cedar Creek, too. What had opened in midsummer as a hopeful effort evaporated away with shocking swiftness as Union forces overwhelmed Early's bedraggled Confederates even as they'd been on the cusp of victory.

The wounded Ramseur was captured later that night while traveling in an ambulance with the retreating army. He was taken to Belle Grove plantation, which was serving as Phil Sheridan's headquarters. In keeping with the brother-versus-brother symbolism of the American Civil War, a few old friends from West Point stopped by to pay their respects. George Custer, Wesley Merritt, and Henry DuPont—all Union officers—sat or spoke with Ramseur as he lay dying that night. The North Carolinian was in severe pain, once expressing to DuPont, "you don't know how I suffer."

Ramseur wanted the fact to be known that he "died a Christian and had done his duty." His fervent wish was that he could see his precious Nellie one more time and meet just once his little child.

Unfortunately this was not to be. Ramseur died the following morning, October 20, 1864. He was 27 years old. He had been married one week short of one year.

The Confederacy had even less time to live.

Ramseur was mortally wounded during the culminating action of the Valley Campaign's final battle. (wrhs)

"NO TRUER OR NOBLER SPIRIT HAS BEEN SACRIFICED."

The Back Door of Invasion

CHAPTER ONE
SUMMER 1864

Jubal Early was a day late.

Washington D.C. was laid out before him and his small army in the late-July sun. Early could even see the dome of the Capitol. It beckoned to him: attack!

But instead of lightly manned fortifications, the parapets around the city were, according to Early, "lined with troops." The fort to his immediate front, known as Fort Stevens, was bustling with Yankees. His army—which had conducted long marches, a pitched battle two days previously at Monocacy, and then another forced march to Washington—was exhausted.

Prudently, Early called off the assault.

Although unable to capture or seriously threaten the city, Early did take some solace from the attempt. "Major, we haven't taken Washington, but we scared Abe Lincoln like hell," he remarked to an officer soon after leaving the outskirts.

President Abraham Lincoln and his general in chief, Lt. Gen. Ulysses S. Grant, would soon draw up plans to make sure Early or any other Confederates would never scare "Abe Lincoln" and Washington again.

After the Union defeat at New Market in mid-May, Maj. Gen. David Hunter had taken over command of Union forces in the Shenandoah Valley. Hunter promptly moved up the Valley and threatened the vitally important railroad depot of Lynchburg.

This Federal presence forced Gen. Robert E. Lee, commander of the Confederate Army of Northern Virginia, to act. Locked in a continuous struggle with Union armies around Richmond, Lee dispatched his most trusted subordinate, Lt. Gen. Jubal Early, to rescue the city. By railroad and by marching, Early and his Second Corps arrived in the nick of time and defeated the Yankees on June 17-18, 1864. The victory sent

Fort Stevens, which guarded the approach to Washington, D.C., from the north along the 7th Street Pike (now Georgia Avenue) was named for slain Union Brig. Gen. Isaac Stevens. Stevens, who had been a U.S. Congressman and the first governor of Washington Territory, was killed at the battle of Chantilly in September of 1862.
Fort Stevens was one of 68 forts that ring the capital. Altogether, the fortifications defending Washington boasted an armament of 905 guns-with placements for 600 more. (pg)

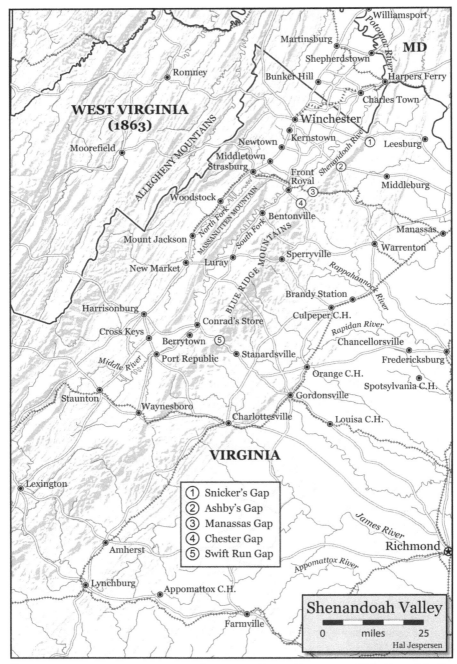

THE AREA OF OPERATIONS FOR THE AUTUMN SHENANDOAH VALLEY CAMPAIGN OF 1864—Framed by the Allegheny Mountains to the west and the Blue Ridge Mountains to the east, with Massanutten Mountain running down part of its center, the Shenandoah Valley had seen significant action in the spring of 1862. It continued to bedevil the Federal government at the Confederates' "back door of invasion." Grant finally addressed the problem after the impotent Confederate run on Washington in late July of 1864.

Hunter scurrying into the mountains and cleared the path for Early to march to the Potomac River.

At the head of "Stonewall" Jackson's old command, Early did just that, taking the war from Lynchburg to the gates of Washington.

Understandably, with the presidential election looming in the fall, Lincoln could not let such an invasion happen, especially on the high-profile heels of previous Confederate incursions across the Potomac, which had each set off waves of fear and panic across the North. Coupled with the high casualty figures from Grant's Overland campaign—the Federal effort to destroy Lee's army that spring—popular support for the war in the North was beginning to wane. If Lincoln hoped to win reelection, the elimination of the Shenandoah Valley as an invasion route would have to be a top priority.

Known as the "Breadbasket of the Confederacy," the lush Valley stretched from Lynchburg in the south to Winchester in the north, bracketed by the Blue Ridge Mountains to the east and the Alleghany Mountains to the west. Running like a spine through the Valley is Massanutten Mountain. It begins east of Harrisonburg and continues for 71 miles until leveling off south of Middletown. This mountain dissects the larger valley into two smaller valleys: the Shenandoah and Luray.

The main thoroughfare through the Shenandoah Valley was the Valley Turnpike. Harrisonburg, Strasburg,

The Shenandoah Valley not only offered some of the most scenic landscapes in Virginia, it also served a vital role as "the Breadbasket of the Confederacy." (dd/pg)

In June, Maj. Gen. David Hunter was the latest in a string of Federal commanders to come to grief after operating in the Valley. (loc)

Maj. Gen. George B. McClellan, the former commander of the Army of the Potomac (top), Maj. Gen. George Gordon Meade, its current commander (below), and Maj. Gen. William B. Franklin (bottom) were among those considered to command the new Union army in the Shenandoah. (loc)

New Market, and Middletown sat astride it. Railroad lines also ran into and through the region. The Shenandoah River, the main water source for the Valley, flowed from south to north. Thus, if an individual traveled north from Lynchburg to Winchester, they were going "down the Valley;" people heading south from Winchester were going "up."

Because of its geography, the Valley made a perfect "back door" for invasion. In 1863, Lee had used the Valley as an avenue of advance, emerging from the mountain ranges in Pennsylvania. The campaign culminated in the battle of Gettysburg, which left more than 50,000 casualties. The extreme loss of life provided the backdrop for President Lincoln's "Gettysburg Address." The president hoped that these men "had not died in vain."

Now, a year later, Early had reached the doorsteps of Washington using that same route. Only the delaying action at Monocacy, which would eventually become known as "The Battle that Saved Washington," prevented Early's Confederates from slipping into the city. This back door of invasion had to be closed.

Unfortunately, after the Southern legions marched away from Washington, the Union response was anything but decisive. One of the issues was the confusing problem of authority. The Federals had departmentalized different regions. Four military departments embracing Washington, Maryland, Pennsylvania, and the Shenandoah Valley needed to be merged into one. These departments had different commanders, and coordination in an orderly manner was difficult to achieve—and so, after threatening Washington, Early slipped back to the Valley unopposed.

After the failed pursuit of the Confederates, Grant had to appoint a new commander who would have authority over all the departments and be responsible for destroying Early's army.

Under consideration were Maj. Gen. William B. Franklin; former commander of the Army of the Potomac, Maj. Gen. George B. McClellan; and the current commander of the Army of the Potomac, Maj. Gen. George G. Meade. President Lincoln and Secretary of War Edwin Stanton balked at all three propositions.

McClellan's name had been floated as a possible ploy to keep him from running against Lincoln for president in the fall. However, his contentious relationship with Lincoln and one-time political ally Stanton almost assured more of the same sorts of problems and delays that had led to McClellan's removal from command a year and a half earlier. Nor could Lincoln afford the other edge of that sword—on the outside chance that McClellan performed well, it would only bolster Little

With his attention focused on the trench warfare around Petersburg, Lt. Gen. Ulysses S. Grant needed a subordinate with an aggressive spirit to spearhead operations in the Shenandoah Valley. (loc)

Mac's bid for the White House. The next candidate, Franklin, was passed over because of the lackluster record he'd amassed with the Army of the Potomac earlier in the war. Meade, too, was rejected; Lincoln was holding back political forces wishing to have the Army of the Potomac commander replaced, and the president did not want to appear as though he was appeasing the opposition.

Finally, Grant proposed Meade's chief of cavalry, Maj. Gen. Philip Sheridan. Lincoln and Stanton again had their reservations, but time was of the essence, and they acquiesced. On August 6, Grant and Sheridan met outside Frederick, Maryland, at Monocacy Station. There, Grant handed his subordinate written orders for the task ahead. The two men departed in opposite directions; time would tell if they were also starting on diverging destinies.

*   *   *

The campaign waged in the Shenandoah Valley that year would take on a greater significance than its sister campaign two years earlier. In the spring of 1862,

Grant and Sheridan met at the Monocacy rail station outside Frederick, Maryland. (wrhs)

Confederate Maj. Gen. Thomas Stonewall Jackson used the geography of the Valley to influence Union strategy in Virginia. Jackson's victories at Front Royal, Winchester, Cross Keys, and Port Republic managed to keep reinforcements from being sent to Maj. Gen. George McClellan's Union army advancing on Richmond.

In 1864, the outcome would have an impact on the entire Union war effort itself. With operations there taking place on the eve of the November elections, any adverse outcome in the Valley could influence the Northern populace as they went to the polls to cast their ballot for the next president of the United States. Although Atlanta had fallen in early September, improving Lincoln's chances for reelection, Virginia still remained a focal point. With Grant and Meade bogged down in front of Richmond and Petersburg, all eyes were on the Valley. A major Union defeat there could counterbalance the gains achieved by Maj. Gen. William T. Sherman in Georgia.

This could not have been comforting to Abraham Lincoln or the rest of the Union high command. The Shenandoah Valley was a place where Union hopes had been dashed in the past, and there was nothing to indicate that this time things would be different.

For the Southern cause, the Valley had been a scene of pride and victory. During the summer of 1864, Jubal Early had used the region to threaten Washington. If he could maintain a tight hold on the Shenandoah, the advantages to the South would be numerous. The Confederates could continue to threaten northward, force the detachment of additional Union troops to the region and thus weaken the grip on Richmond and Petersburg, and continue the production of materials and produce essential to the war effort. Stonewall Jackson's words "If the Valley is lost so is Virginia" could not have been more prophetic two years later.

With a new cast of characters, the Valley would take

center stage again in the fall of 1864. The rolling hills and flats between the Alleghenies and the Massanutten would play a crucial role in the coming drama. During this act, the region would witness something yet to be seen in that part of Virginia: the concept of total war. Consequences of defeat would be disastrous to either side. The outcome of the great struggle that had plagued the nation was on the line.

Lt. Gen. Jubal Early, C.S.A. (left) and Maj. Gen. Phil Sheridan, U.S.A. (right) led the Shenandoah armies that would clash throughout the bloody autumn. (loc)

As Jubal Early studied Washington's defenses outside Fort Stevens, President Lincoln stood inside the fort, studying Early's Confederates. His stovepipe hat made him a noticeable target, and soon Lincoln came under fire—only the second time a sitting president had been fired upon during wartime (Madison, during the War of 1812, was the first). The site, now maintained by the NPS, is near Georgia Avenue at 13th Street and Quackenbos Street NW. (pg)

"Little Phil" and "Old Jube"

CHAPTER TWO

SUMMER 1864

Philip H. Sheridan was not physically impressive. Standing at 5'5", many of his peers towered above him. President Lincoln, an astute observer with a flair for description, called him a "brown, chunky little chap, with a long body, short legs, not enough neck to hang him, and such arms that if his ankles itch he can scratch them without stooping." Sheridan's contemporaries also remembered his oddly shaped head. Perhaps to hide this feature, Sheridan more often than not wore his hat at an angle.

Yet inside this small frame, there burned a fiery ambition that was fueled by a hair-trigger temper and a strong will to succeed, no matter what the cost. "You will find him big enough for the purpose before we get through with him," Grant once said of him.

Sheridan was 33 years old when he was selected to command the Army of the Shenandoah. It was for this reason, age, that President Lincoln and Secretary Stanton were hesitant to approve his appointment.

Their new army commander grew up in the hamlet of Somerset, Ohio, in the eastern part of the state. In 1848, he was appointed to West Point. Suspended for a year for an altercation with a fellow cadet, Sheridan finally graduated in the Class of 1853. His antebellum service was monotonous, and promotions were slow. By the fall of 1861, when he headed east to participate in the War of Rebellion, he had risen to the rank of captain.

Promoted to brigadier general in September 1862, "Little Phil" led an infantry division at Perryville, Stones River, and Chickamauga. For his actions at Stones River, Sheridan was promoted to major general. In November 1863, Sheridan led the assault on Missionary Ridge that broke the siege of Chattanooga. These actions did not go unnoticed by Maj. Gen. Ulysses S. Grant. The following March, Grant was promoted to lieutenant general and

After passing away on August 5, 1888, Phil Sheridan, a full general, was buried at Arlington National Cemetery, slightly down the slope from Arlington House (pictured in the background). The grave marker only reads "Sheridan," but buried there also are his wife, brother, son, and daughters. (pg)

Sheridan spearheaded the assault to take Missionary Ridge and break the Siege of Chattanooga in November 1863. (loc)

The Trevilian Station battlefield, where Sheridan's cavalry was turned back during a raid in June 1864. (dd)

made general in chief of the Federal armies. Coming to Virginia to direct operations, Grant brought Little Phil with him and gave him command of the cavalry corps of the Army of the Potomac.

This assignment did not fit well. Sheridan botched the opening maneuvers of the spring campaign when he failed to cover the army's right flank—a failure that ultimately led to the two-day bloodbath in the Wilderness. After the battle, he failed to secure the army's route to Spotsylvania Court House. This debacle completely soured his relationship with the commander of the Army of the Potomac, Maj. Gen. George G. Meade.

On May 8, a meeting between the two quickly escalated into a fiery verbal confrontation. Surprisingly, this did not result in Sheridan's censure. Instead, Grant sent Sheridan with his entire corps southward to engage the Confederate cavalry. Although Sheridan could count the May 11 battle of Yellow Tavern and the death of Maj. Gen. J. E. B. Stuart as a victory, the day following the engagement, he was nearly surrounded and trapped outside Richmond. In June, Sheridan and two of his divisions were stopped by Stuart's successor, Maj. Gen. Wade Hampton, during a raid on the Virginia Central Railroad at Trevilian Station.

In short, Virginia had not been kind to Phil Sheridan. His shortcomings were apparent. Any misgivings about his abilities on the part of other officers within the army may have been kept private so as not to offend the temperamental Sheridan or the proud general in chief Grant.

Grant probably also understood that, due to the catastrophe on the march to Spotsylvania, Sheridan could not work with Meade. It may not have been due to Sheridan's past successes, then, but rather his recent failures, that Grant recommended him to command the Army of the Shenandoah.

When Sheridan assumed his new command, he had more than 40,000 men in all three branches to put in the field against Jubal Early. His men came from a range of states, including Pennsylvania, New York, Massachusetts, West Virginia, and Iowa. The foundation of the army was the battle-tested VI Corps from the Army of the Potomac, led by Maj. Gen. Horatio Wright.

Wright relied on the combined experience of division commanders David A. Russell, George W. Getty, and James B. Ricketts—all of them brigadiers. Russell had begun the conflict as a colonel and rose through the ranks. Getty had held various posts during the early years of the war and was wounded at the Wilderness. Ricketts had been fighting for the Union cause since First Manassas. The backbone of the corps was a brigade from Getty's division. Made up of six regiments from Vermont, these men were some of the best-disciplined and hardest fighting men the North had to offer.

Sheridan could also call upon the XIX Corps from the Army of the Gulf, commanded by Maj. Gen. William Emory. Like Wright, Emory also had two veteran division commanders, Brig. Gen. William Dwight and Brig. Gen. Cuvier Grover. Both had seen service in Virginia earlier in the war, and Dwight had been wounded at the battle of Williamsburg, in May 1862.

Upon arriving in the Valley, Sheridan also inherited the Army of West Virginia. As its name implied, this unit consisted mainly of men from the newly formed state. It was commanded by one of Sheridan's roommates at West Point, Maj. Gen. George Crook. Colonels Isaac Duval and Joseph Thoburn led the divisions. Both were experienced fighters.

VI Corps commander Maj. Gen. Horatio Wright (loc)

Twelve batteries of artillery supported the Army of the Shenandoah. Directing the guns attached to the Army of West Virginia was Capt. Henry DuPont. DuPont had graduated first in the West Point Class of May 1861 just after the war began. At New Market, DuPont had distinguished himself by using his batteries to cover the retreat of the Union army.

Three divisions of cavalry were assigned to the army, led by Bvt. Maj. Gen. Alfred T. A. Torbert. Brigadier Generals William W. Averell, Wesley Merritt, and James Wilson commanded these divisions. Averell had fought at Hartwood Church, Kelly's Ford, and Droop Mountain. Merritt's solid service with the U.S. Regulars had earned him a general's star on the eve of the battle of Gettysburg. Wilson, like his army commander, had come to the eastern army in the spring of 1864.

Sheridan (standing, center) surrounded by members of his staff: Henry Davies, Wes Merritt, James Wilson, Al Torbert and David Gregg (loc)

Although the VI Corps formed its nucleus, the army's greatest asset was the cavalry. The role of the Union cavalry had changed drastically since the war began. By the autumn of 1864, these troopers had transitioned from scouts and escorts to a mounted strike force. The horse was no longer a means of transportation—it was a source of mobility used to move armed men from point to point. Many in the ranks were armed with the repeating seven-shot Spencer carbine and were augmented by batteries of horse artillery. These factors made Sheridan's troopers more than capable of contending with their gray counterparts. It also put them on a superior plain when confronted by enemy infantry.

That enemy army was commanded by the colorful "Old Jube." Along with the moniker "My Bad Old Man," Early had two of the most fitting nicknames given to any leader outside of "Stonewall" in the Confederate military. Both of his nicknames were well-deserved. He had a short temper, was not immune to using an array of swear words, and was a fearless combat leader. Part of his cantankerous temper can be traced to suffering

Early's counterattack at Prospect Hill during the battle of Fredericksburg helped to stabilize the Confederate line during the battle. (dd/pg)

from severe arthritis. General Robert E. Lee was credited with giving Early the second of his two monikers, "My Bad Old Man," as Early was the only officer with the nerve to curse in the presence of the Southern leader. Lee purportedly overlooked Early's profanity because the "Bad Old Man" fought so well.

The irascible Early was born on November 3, 1816, in Franklin County to a wealthy and well-connected Virginia family. He attended academies at both Danville and Lynchburg in preparation for his entry into West Point in 1833.

While attending the academy, an argument with future Confederate Brig. Gen. Lewis Armistead escalated to the point that Early had a plate smashed over his head. Armistead resigned instead of facing the chance of dismissal. Early continued on, and upon graduation in 1837, he fought in the Seminole War before resigning in 1838.

After his resignation, Early studied law and began a practice in Rocky Mount, Virginia. He would return to the army in January 1847 as a major in command of Virginia volunteers during the Mexican-American War.

When Virginia seceded, Early entered Confederate service, receiving the rank of colonel of the 24th Virginia Infantry, which he led at the battle of First Manassas. He received his brigadier general commission shortly thereafter due to the role he and his regiment played in this first major battle.

Early was wounded at the battle of Williamsburg, but after his recuperation, he participated in every engagement of the Army of Northern Virginia. He earned promotion to the rank of major general in January 1863 and to lieutenant general in May 1864. When Lt. Gen. Richard Ewell was ordered to oversee the defenses of Richmond in May 1864, Early succeeded him as commander of the Second Corps.

By September 1864, Early's Army of the Valley numbered approximately 13,000 men. The infantry and artillery accounted for 9,000 while the cavalry comprised the rest. Confederate veteran G. H. Baskett gave the following description of a typical Confederate soldier:

A face browned by exposure and heavily bearded . . . begrimed with dust and sweat, marked here and there with the darker stains of powder . . . a frame tough and sinewy, and trained by hardship to surprising powers of endurance. Above this an old wool hat, worn, and weather beaten . . . over a soiled shirt, which is unbuttoned and buttonless at the collar, is a ragged gray jacket that does not reach the hips, with sleeves inches too short. Below this trousers of a non-descript color, without form and almost void, are held in place by a leather belt to which is attached the cartridge box . . . and the bayonet scabbard . . . dirty socks-disappear in a pair of badly used and curiously contorted shoes.

For a large number of the Virginians in Early's command, the return to the Shenandoah Valley was a homecoming. Most had fought in the Valley campaign of 1862. More than half of the Virginia regiments were recruited entirely or in part from the Valley region. These men could be counted on to go above and beyond because they were truly defending "home and hearth."

The soldiers had trust in Old Jube. An artillerist pronounced Early as "without a superior in the Army of Northern Virginia" on the eve of the campaign. A Georgia private probably spoke for countless others when he wrote, "Expect a glorious victory for us—the 'Old Guard.' God be with the right."

Leading the "Old Guard" were some of the best commanders in the Confederate service. Major General John C. Breckinridge, a former vice president of the United States, commanded one corps. His divisions were headed by Maj. Gen. John Gordon and Brig. Gen. Gabriel C. Wharton. Wharton had escaped from Fort Donelson in February 1862 and had seen extensive service in the Valley and western Virginia. One of the notable brigades in Wharton's division was commanded by Col. George S. Patton, grandfather of Gen. George S. Patton of World War II fame.

Gordon was the only division commander in the Army of the Valley who had not attended a military college prior to the war. Besides a brigade of Georgians, his division consisted of the consolidated remnants of the old "Stonewall Brigade" and "Louisiana Tigers." To balance his force after Lynchburg, Early had temporarily assigned Gordon's division to Breckinridge's command. Later, in the middle of September, Breckinridge would be transferred to organize Confederate forces in southwestern Virginia and Gordon would return to the Second Corps.

Along with Gordon, Early could rely on two other experienced division commanders in the Second Corps, Maj. Gens. Robert E. Rodes and Stephen D. Ramseur. The former was promoted to the rank after Chancellorsville and performed well at Spotsylvania Court House. Coincidentally, Ramseur had been wounded at both battles.

The artillery supporting the army consisted of five battalions and was commanded initially by Brig. Gen. Armistead L. Long. Attached to the army were 4,500 to 5,000 cavalry commanded by Maj. Gen. Fitzhugh Lee. A nephew of Gen. Robert E. Lee, Fitz was a protégé of the late Maj. Gen. J. E. B. Stuart.

On these men, Early would lean in the hopes of recapturing past glory.

Maj. Gen. John C. Breckenridge (loc)

Maj. Gen. John Brown Gordon (loc)

Brig. Gen. Gabriel C. Wharton (loc)

Opening Maneuvers

CHAPTER THREE
AUGUST-SEPTEMBER 1864

After parting company with Grant at Monocacy Station, Phil Sheridan set off to the Shenandoah Valley to see the command he was to lead. He was headed to the theater where Confederates had always held court. On August 9, VI Corps brigade commander Brig. Gen. Emory Upton wrote to his sister, "A new campaign will be inaugurated tomorrow . . . . [H]ow soon it may develop . . . what may be its consequences no one knows but I trust it will be successful."

The next morning, August 10, the campaign began in earnest. The Army of the Shenandoah struck out south, headed for Berryville, Virginia, 20 miles away. The march to this small hamlet east of Winchester was an effort to dislodge the Confederates from their position near Bunker Hill.

Confederate Brig. Gen. John Imboden, who had gained a favorable reputation the previous year when overseeing the wagon-train of wounded Confederates from Gettysburg, had been monitoring Union preparations in the lower Valley. He sent a report to Early, dated August 9—the same day Sheridan left Monocacy Station. Imboden reported that "a large force had been concentrated at Harper's Ferry, consisting of the VI, IXX, and Crook's corps . . . and that it was moving towards Berryville," Early later recalled.

The intelligence gained by Imboden's troopers and the subsequent Yankee movement prompted Early to retire from his position around Bunker Hill. Early ordered a "movement from Bunker Hill to the east of Winchester to cover the roads from Charlestown and Berryville to that place."

Sheridan's maneuver had the desired effect. Within days, the Federals encamped south of Middletown along the banks of Cedar Creek. The Confederates lay some

Harper's Ferry National Historical Park maintains the 1860s charm of the village. Located at the confluence of the Potomac and Shenandoah Rivers and home to a prewar arsenal, Harper's Ferry proved strategically important but tactically impossible to hold. As a result, it changed hands multiple times during the war. (cm)

Harper's Ferry, where Sheridan first met the Army of the Shenandoah (pg)

eight miles to the south, ensconced atop Fisher's Hill. Approximately 10 miles separated the opposing forces.

The two armies sat directly across from one another from August 12 to August 14. During this time, Sheridan attempted to develop his enemy's position. The probes against the Confederates were minor and resulted in desultory fighting. Late on the afternoon of August 14, Sheridan received a dispatch from Grant informing him that a Confederate force had left the siege lines around Richmond and Petersburg. These Rebels were bound for the Valley. This additional force would even the numerical odds.

With Sheridan leading, the Army of the Shenandoah pursued Early's army up the Valley. (loc)

The force that Grant informed Sheridan about were elements from the Confederate First Corps under the command of Lt. Gen. Richard Anderson. On August 6, General Lee dispatched Maj. Gen. Joseph Kershaw's infantry division and Maj. Wilfred Cutshaw's artillery battalion to the Valley. In addition, Lee also sent the cavalry division under his nephew, Maj. Gen. Fitzhugh Lee. With these reinforcements, Lee hoped that Early could capture the initiative from the Federals.

On August 14, Anderson's men began arriving in Front Royal. Anderson had received communication from Lee on August 12 providing information that Early had fallen back from Newtown toward Fisher's Hill, as Sheridan's forces threatened his right flank, approximately 15 miles to Fisher's Hill. Believing that Sheridan might attempt to gain Early's rear, Lee directed Anderson to resume his march. Circumstances would

dictate his approach. At all times, Anderson was to have frequent communication with Early.

However, at Anderson's approach, Sheridan elected to march north, down the Valley, to find a more suitable defensive position. The withdrawal negated the maneuvering of the last week as the Federals began their march to Halltown, just south of Harper's Ferry. All in all, the withdrawal took around six days, and by August 22, Sheridan reached his destination. Due to the time they'd already spent in the area, one soldier compared the army to a popular newspaper, coining it "Harper's Weekly."

The marching to and fro also had an effect on the Confederates. One soldier from Alabama had a pet dog named Collins. When his division commander, Maj. Gen. Robert Rodes rode through the camp one day, he inquired about the dog's whereabouts. The soldier did not know but took the moment to compare the current campaign with the dog's habits. "Every morning Custer, or some other Yankee comes galloping down the road with cavalry," the Alabamian said, "and you [Rodes] go after them as hard as you can split, and you haven't cotched a single cavalryman yet, and Collins [the dog], every time a train passes shoots out after it, and she ain't cotched narry train yet. You and Collins just alike."

*   *   *

The Federal and Confederate forces continued their waltz through the end of August. Early moved back to Bunker Hill and Sheridan marched to Charlestown. On September 3, the Army of the Shenandoah marched to Berryville. The next few days were spent building and improving on a line of earthworks that stretched for some eight miles.

This strong posture on the part of Federals exhibited Sheridan's desire to remain on the defensive. Although he still outnumbered his opponent, Sheridan felt that an attack

Sheridan's army withdrawing from Strasburg. (wrhs)

and the risk of defeat outweighed any reward. The feeling seemingly intensified with word that the Federal armies under Maj. Gen. William T. Sherman had captured the vital southern city of Atlanta, Georgia. Any setback suffered by Sheridan would nullify Sherman's gains.

Sheridan's mindset began to change when word reached the Union camp that Anderson's force was returning to Petersburg. Word of the Rebel departure was indeed confirmed by two Winchester citizens. This sudden turn of events convinced him that it was now time to act. The two armies had stood staring at each other for the better part of two weeks, and it now seemed that fortune was beginning to tilt in Sheridan's favor. First, though, he had to convince Grant that his offensive plan was sound.

The general in chief viewed the fall of Atlanta differently, however, and he would have preferred that Sheridan follow up the victory in Georgia with a grand offensive in Virginia. When none came, Grant took it upon himself to visit his lieutenant. Just as they had met a month earlier, the two met in person again, this time at Charlestown. There, Grant approved Sheridan's plan to move the Army of the Shenandoah south from Berryville to Newtown and turn the Confederate flank. Once again, the two men parted ways—Grant with an understanding of Sheridan's strategy and Sheridan with an understanding of his superior's expectations.

Within just a few days of their meeting, though, Sheridan altered his plan. This came about due to intelligence from Brig. Gen. William Averell. Averell's cavalry had confirmed that Early had sent two divisions to Stephenson's Depot, north of Winchester. The maneuver

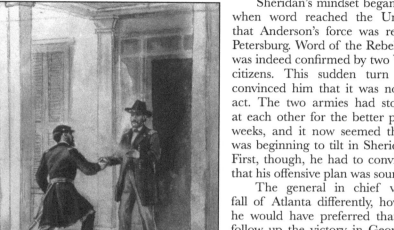

On September 17, Grant and Sheridan met in Charlestown so the commanding general could reiterate his expectations. (wrhs)

Alfred Waud sketched the September movements of the army. (loc)

had left the Confederates strung out and vulnerable to being attacked and annihilated in detail. Rather than moving to Newtown as originally envisioned, Sheridan decided to march directly to Winchester in the hope that he could catch Early's forces separated and defeat them piecemeal.

Supplemental orders went out late on the night of September 18 directing the army to be prepared to move the next morning. The Army of the Shenandoah would be marching to battle for the first time. Would this Union force have better luck than their predecessors?

The Union army marched through Charlestown. (wrhs)

Third Winchester,
Part I

CHAPTER FOUR
SEPTEMBER 19, 1864

Speed: that was the key element in Sheridan's plan and the key to having the chance to destroy Early. Little Phil planned to move his army across Opequon Creek, through the Berryville Canyon, and assault Maj. Gen. Stephen Ramseur's division near Winchester. He hoped to dispose of Ramseur and then chew up the rest of Early's divisions piecemeal as they attempted to come to Ramseur's aid.

Although the plan was simple, it involved risks. Rebel pickets were posted along the western bank of the Opequon to contest a Union advance. The canyon itself also served as a potential hazard. With a narrow road and steep sides, the gorge had the semblance of a funnel. Only one Federal unit could pass through at a time. Any strong resistance by the Rebels or slow movement through the gorge by the Federals had the potential to shatter Sheridan's strategy.

Before sunrise, the Army of the Shenandoah stirred. James Wilson's cavalry division led the advance on the Berryville Turnpike. The troopers were to force their way across the creek, through the canyon, and establish a foothold in the open ground beyond. Two veteran regiments from New York took the lead.

Brig. Gen. James Wilson (loc)

Ramseur's division, numbering around 2,000 muskets, were all that stood between the Yankee cavalry and Winchester. The rest of Early's army was marching rapidly back to Winchester from a march to Bunker Hill the day before. It would be up to Ramseur to hold off Wilson's thrust until the rest of the army could consolidate. Immediately opposing the Federal cavalry was one of Ramseur's brigades, commanded by Brig. Gen. Robert Johnston.

The Pennsylvania Monument in the Winchester National Cemetery was erected in 1890.
(dd/pg)

The Tar Heels gave ground grudgingly as they fell back. As the Union cavalrymen came on, one observer said the North Carolinians "would halt, face to the rear

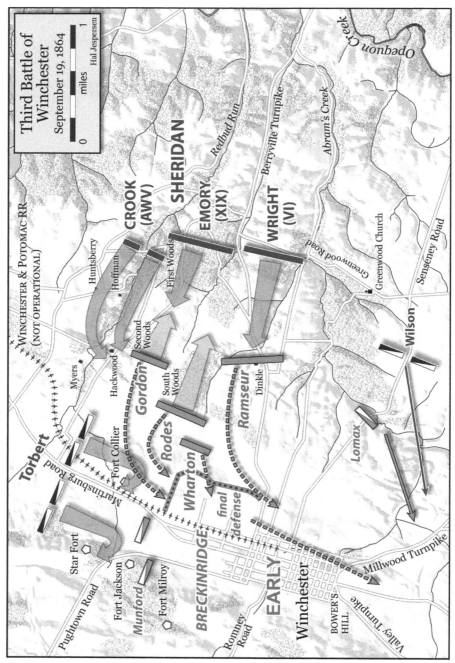

THE FIRST PHASE OF THE BATTLE OF THIRD WINCHESTER—Early's Confederates repulsed Horatio Wright's and William Emory's assaults along the Berryville Turnpike and held Torbert in check above the town. Not until Sheridan ordered George Crook to attack Early's left was the Rebel line forced back to a new position.

The attack of Maj. Gen. James Ricketts' division , north of the Berryville Turnpike. (loc)

rank, wait until the horses got to within 100 yards, and turn and fire."

Ramseur's Confederates did just enough to delay the Federal advance. Shortly before 6 a.m., Sheridan rode through the canyon and ascended a nearby knoll occupied by the J. Eversole farm. Peering behind him through the gorge, he could see his infantry strung out along the road. What the Union commander hoped to avoid was becoming a reality: his wagons, artillery, and infantry had become stacked in the canyon. It would be hours before the jam could be untangled and the infantry brought into line.

If the jam-up in the canyon was not enough to frustrate Little Phil, Jubal Early had brought two of his three remaining infantry divisions, under Maj. Gens. Robert Rodes and John Gordon, onto the field. The first brigade, under Brig. Gen. Bryan Grimes of Rodes' division, deployed to the east of Winchester between 9 a.m. and 10 a.m.

The first Union infantry to arrive was Maj. Gen. Horatio Wright's VI Corps. As they extracted themselves from the Berryville Canyon, the divisions filed into the fields south of the Berryville Pike. Brigadier General George Getty's division deployed first; James Ricketts' men followed, extending the line to the right of the pike. David Russell's division was kept in reserve in column along the road. Ricketts' division extended the line across the pike and linked up with the XIX Corps. Major General William Emory's divisions deployed north of the road.

While the view today is clogged with traffic, Phil Sheridan had an excellent view from this spot to see the disposition of his army as it prepared to attack. (dd/pg)

With the infantry arriving on the field, Wilson moved to the south along the Senseney Road to guard the army's flank where his troopers would spend the rest of the day in sporadic skirmishing.

With dispositions made, Sheridan settled on an all-out assault against the Confederates. The Union line would guide on the Berryville Turnpike.

*   *   *

Early, meanwhile, had pulled Ramseur's division from its forward position to the right of the Confederate infantry line once Rodes and Gordon arrived. Both divisions filed into line next to Ramseur, whose division occupied the right astride the Berryville Pike. Rodes' division occupied the center of the line on Ramseur's left. Gordon connected to Rodes, his left flank resting on Red Bud Run near the Hackwood farm. Confederate cavalry patrolled both flanks. The last of Early's infantry, the division under Maj. Gen. John Breckenridge, had been stopped at Stephenson's Depot to bolster Confederate cavalry responding to Union cavalry incursions north of Winchester.

Around the same time Yankee gunners were ramming home powder and shot for the signal gun that would start their assault, Early directed Breckenridge to bring his men from Stephenson's Depot. The order would deprive his flank of infantry, but the Confederate commander compensated by moving the cavalry division of Maj. Gen. Fitzhugh Lee to the area.

At 11:40 a.m., the Yankee signal cannon fired a single shot, and the attack began.

South of the turnpike, George Getty's division advanced against Stephen Ramseur's men. "Onward through the cornfields and over the grassy knolls . . . the rebel artillery swept with terrible effect . . ." wrote one soldier in the 77th New York. "[T]he long line pressed forward . . . at every step . . . men were dropping, dropping . . . . Now on this side, now on that they fell." An officer from Rhode Island observing the attack wrote grimly that "artillery was used freely on both sides."

Surging ahead on Getty's right was the veteran Vermont brigade. The Confederates opened fire just as the Vermonters reached a bend where the turnpike veered sharply to the south. Taking advantage of the terrain for cover, the Green Mountain Boys moved into

The position occupied by Gordon's men (dd/pg)

a ravine south of the road. Colonels William Emerson and J. Warren Keifer, commanding the brigades of Ricketts' division, may not have seen the Vermonters disappear into the swale. Advancing through the fields on Getty's right, they continued to march straight for the Confederates as they passed the bend in the road. These combined maneuvers effectively caused a gap to open and then widen on the Federal line.

Robert Rodes, killed instantly by a Federal shot, was loaded onto an ambulance. His death "shook the whole corps," a subordinate said. (wrhs)

Across the fields around Winchester stood "some of the finest troops in the South," one observer said. Combined with "intrepid use of artillery," the outnumbered yet proud Second Corps gave the Union assault pause. Then, like assaults of old, the Second Corps division of Robert Rodes readied for a counterattack.

To spearhead his attack, Rodes looked to Brig. Gen. Cullen Battle's Alabama brigade. He trusted these men from the Deep South. He had marched to war in 1861 at the head of one of the regiments. As the brigade commander waved his men forward to the attack, Rodes sat calmly on his black stallion, shouting, "Charge them, boys!"

At that instant, a Federal artillery shell exploded overhead and the division commander leaned slightly forward then crumpled to the ground dead. Even today, it is unclear whether a shell or bullet caused the fatal wound, but what is certain is that Early and the Confederate army suffered an irreplaceable loss. Battle wrote that Rodes' death "shook the whole corps," and

A monument marks the location on the Third Winchester battlefield where Robert Rodes was killed. After his death, Rodes's body was brought back to his native Lynchburg, Virginia, and buried in the Presbyterian cemetery. His brother, Virginius, who served as his adjutant throughout the war, was eventually buried beside him. (pg)

The death of Brig. Gen. David Russell. A soldier in the 121st New York lamented that "we lost another of our famous and gallant commanders." (wrhs)

Brig. Gen. Emory Upton earned his stars in May of 1864 after employing innovative tactics during the battle of Spotsylvania Court House. He would go on to be one of the most influential military thinkers of the century. (loc)

"the whole army mourned his death. No single death—save that of Jackson, caused such deep regret."

The time for eulogizing Rodes would come later. His division, left in the dark about the tragedy that befell their beloved commander, drove home the counterattack. As luck would have it, the Confederates, advancing rapidly, aimed exactly for the gap in the Federal line. The fight became a stand-up affair. Veteran soldiers on both sides worked like machines, loading, firing, then reloading. The accuracy and rate of fire from the Confederates is evident by the tales of Union soldiers. One Pennsylvanian remembered the Southerners' fire doing "great execution to our line."

Back on Eversole's Knoll, Sheridan watched in horror as the magnificent hole opened on his front and Battle's brigade advanced straight for it. The situation spelled doom for his army. The only reserve close at hand was Wright's only uncommitted division, commanded by David Russell. Russell reacted quickly and immediately began to bring the brigades of Cols. Oliver Edwards and Edward Campbell to the field. A soldier in the 49th Pennsylvania remembered that Russell rode to the skirmish line, remarking "something must be done quick" to halt the enemy advance. While superintending the deployment of his men, Russell was struck by an exploding piece of shrapnel and died instantly.

Russell's actions before his death helped save the army, though, by blunting the Confederate counterattack.

The Federal line extended into the First Woods (left) and then advanced from the woods across open fields (below) toward the Confederate position. (dd/pg)

As his brigades engaged the enemy, he dispatched the brigade of Brig. Gen. Emory Upton to move around the right of his line. Upton led his men beyond the flank and faced to the left. From there, he was in a perfect position to advance against the Confederate left. "General Upton gave the order . . . and crash went that volley of lead and down tumbled those brave fellows," wrote a soldier from the 121st New York. "'Forward charge' rang out Upton's short, incisive command, and away we went. Reaching the point where their line had stood, we saw many of them lying there . . . at once out rushed our companion regiments in fine order." This counterthrust managed to push the Confederates back, and the two lines stabilized.

North of the road, William Emory's assault had not fared much better. As his men exited the Berryville Canyon, Emory directed them to extend the Union line into a thicket known as the First Woods. Brigadier General Cuvier Grover's division held the right of the line. Brigadier General William Dwight held the left and connected with Ricketts' division.

When the Sixth Corps divisions of George Getty and J. Warren Keifer advanced at the sound of the signal cannon, Emory's Yankees emerged from the woods and stepped out into an open field. "[T]he lines advanced over a country much broken and quite densely wooded," Grover wrote. One Yankee remembered that they were "subjected to a destructive fire of musketry, grape and canister." Ahead of them was another thicket, known as the Second Woods, and Grover's troops headed straight for it, driving Rebel skirmishers before them.

As Federal casualties mounted during the advance, the Confederate line wavered and then, to Gordon's dismay, the Georgia brigade broke and streamed toward the rear. As the division commander spurred to rally the broken brigade and stave off a rippling effect, the Confederates were saved by their artillery, double-loaded with canister to discourage the Union advance.

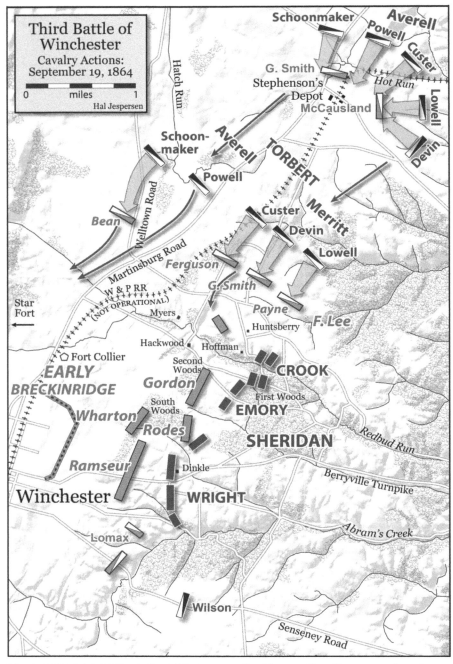

Third Battle of Winchester
Cavalry Actions:
September 19, 1864

0 ——— miles ——— 1

Hal Jespersen

LATER PHASE OF THE BATTLE OF THIRD WINCHESTER—Crook's assault and the progessive advance of the Union cavalry set the stage for the second and final phase of the battle. The Union attack was spearheaded by Averell's and Torbert's cavalry. The Federal troopers crashed into the Confederate line. Combined with an all-out infantry advance, Early's army collapsed and retreated through Winchester.

Grover's attack reached the Second Woods but could go no farther. Gordon provided the inspiration to turn the rout of his men into a poignant offensive juggernaut. As one veteran remembered, "what words Gordon had for his men . . . went unrecorded, but his veterans hit the mass of Federals like a hammer."

Prior to the assault, Grover had formed his four brigades into two lines with two brigades each. As Gordon's veterans broke up the first line, the retreating brigades of Cols. Henry Birge and Jacob Sharpe slammed into the second line to escape the onrushing Confederates. The division collapsed, and the men scampered back toward the First Woods. They were greeted by Emory. The corps commander tried in vain to rally his men even as Gordon's men advanced into the open field between the First and Second Woods.

Fortunately, William Dwight's division was ready for Gordon. Advancing out of the woods, the brigades of Cols. George Beal and James McMillan greeted the Rebels with a stifling volley. It was now time for the Confederates to withdraw as Gordon's men were pushed back to the Second Woods. Dwight's division followed, advancing through the wreckage of the field between the woods. There, the Federal line halted, with both sides content to shoot at each other from long range.

The seesaw fighting over the ground north of the Berryville Turnpike was over, and so was the grand Union offensive. If Little Phil wished to salvage the day, he would have to rely on Maj. Gen. George Crook's Army of West Virginia.

Maj. Gen. Cuvier Grover's assault. (loc)

Rutherford B. Hayes, the future 19th president of the United States, charged with his command of Buckeye State men across Redbud Run and up a slope toward where a monument to Ohio now stands. (dd)

Third Winchester,
Part II

CHAPTER FIVE
SEPTEMBER 19, 1864

With the VI and XIX corps fought to a standstill, Sheridan called upon the Army of West Virginia. While many of the regiments were from West Virginia, some of the men hailed from Ohio, Pennsylvania, and Massachusetts. Counted among these troops were veterans of the battle of New Market. Others had seen hard service in the mountains of western Virginia and east Tennessee, thus gaining the moniker the "Mountain Creepers." They called themselves "Crook's Buzzards" after their commander, Maj. Gen. George Crook.

The Buzzards had spent the day back in the Berryville Canyon. In answer to Sheridan's summons, Crook led his men forward through the gorge and directed them into line. First, he sent Col. Joseph Thoburn's division into the First Woods to backstop their comrades. Colonel Isaac Duval's division followed, extending the Union line past a stream called Red Bud Run to the high ground beyond. Crook's deployment of Duval's division was astride the Confederate left flank, with a prime position to turn the enemy line. Crook then dispatched a staff officer, Capt. William McKinley, to instruct Thoburn to advance after Duval's men initiated the assault.

Jubal Early could be proud of the way his Southerners had fought. Greatly outnumbered, the infantry divisions of Stephen Ramseur, John Gordon, and the deceased Robert Rodes had held their own. When the opportunity arose, they had launched devastating counterattacks. Now, across the fields to the west, another Union assault was organizing against them, and Old Jube had to gamble. He called from the left flank John Breckenridge's division, under the direct control of Brig. Gen. Gabriel Wharton, to bolster his line. Wharton would leave behind the brigade of Col. George Patton to support the cavalry. The gamble would not pay off.

Red Bud Run from the Federal approach (dd/pg)

"AN ORDER FOR A

GENERAL FORWARD

MOVEMENT WAS

GIVEN AND AWAY

WE WENT."

— FEDERAL OFFICER

Instead, according to Capt. James Garnett of Rodes' staff, "the withdrawal of this division . . . may be attributed the loss of the day, for now our disasters commenced."

Around 3 p.m., Crook gave the order to attack. The Buzzards went forward with a cheer, down the slope toward Red Bud Run. In some places, the stream had running water but in others the autumn weather had dried it out. "A very destructive fire was opened upon us, in the midst of which our men rushed into and over the creek . . ." cringed Col. Rutherford B. Hayes, leading a brigade in Duval's division. "[A]ll seemed inspired by the right spirit and charged the rebel works pell-mell in the most determined manner."

The Union lines pushed forward, pressing their foe out of the Second Woods. It was here that Crook's divisions joined in; however, the Federals were unable to go on. Despite having abandoned their position, Rodes' and Gordon's Confederates maintained a murderous fire on the Buzzards. The Confederate line was bent, but not broken.

The assault had its desired effect, though, and allowed the Army of the Shenandoah to regain the initiative.

It was now reaching 4 p.m., and the fighting was at a crescendo. Because the XIX Corps was wrecked from the morning's fighting, it would be up to Crook and Wright to win the day. "General Sheridan rode down the line hat in hand, and the whole army cheered and shouted itself hoarse," a Rhode Islander recounted. "An order for a general forward movement was given and away we went." To follow up the Buzzards' success, Sheridan issued orders for a general advance all along his line. Sheridan was putting all his chips on the table.

For the last time that day, the Federals moved forward. All across the fields east of Winchester, the blue infantry pressed the gray—and this time, Little Phil brought to bear a force that would tip the scales in his favor: his mounted divisions.

Earlier that morning, Sheridan ordered the cavalry divisions of Brig. Gens. Wesley Merritt and William Averell to move well beyond the Union right. Their assignment was to either keep the enemy forces north of Winchester occupied while the infantry moved on Ramseur or attack the enemy rear as the situation warranted. Under the overall direction of Maj. Gen. Alfred Torbert, Merritt's division forced a crossing of the Opequon. The brigades of Col. Charles Lowell and Brig. Gen. George A. Custer forded the stream with only token resistance. They were followed by the brigade of Thomas Devin. Several hours after Merritt crossed, Averell's division rode through the tributary to the Valley Pike and headed south.

As Sheridan's infantry engaged their counterparts in the fields around the Berryville Turnpike, the Yankee troopers engaged the Southern cavalrymen holding the Confederate left flank. The Southerners got the best of the better armed and better equipped Yankees. Through dogged skirmishing, they slowed the Federal advance to a crawl. Faced with overwhelming numbers, though, the Confederates had to retreat from Bunker Hill to Stephenson's Depot, but they did so slowly to try and delay the Union cavalry for as long as possible.

Just as Ramseur's division slowed the Yankee advance that morning, so too, did Breckinridge. It would take most of the morning and part of the afternoon before the divisions of Averell and Merritt could join together. When they finally did unite around Stephenson's Depot, though, the Union horsemen presented an intimidating sight. Torbert directed the combined divisions to ride south along the Valley Pike, toward the sound of the guns east of Winchester.

The ground north of Winchester over which the Union cavalry advanced was clear and ideally suited to the maneuvers of mounted soldiers. "The field was open for cavalry operations as the war has not seen," attested Merritt.

Nearing the city, the divisions reached a point just opposite the Rebel fortification known as Fort Collier. The fortification was constructed during the early euphoria of the war in 1861. With bugles blaring, Custer's Michigan brigade led the way. The Union horsemen thundered forward. As the assault struck home, the Confederate line around the fort collapsed under the weight of the mounted charge.

With the lines breaking around Fort Collier and the infantry pressing the Confederates, the weakened Army of the Valley broke under the pressure. Union cavalry thundered forward. Henry Kyd Douglas, who had served with Stonewall Jackson during the 1862 Valley campaign, remembered the Confederates responding with something reminiscent of the Napoleonic age. "For the first time I saw a division of infantry . . . form a hollow square to resist cavalry," he wrote.

During the savage fighting north of Winchester, the great-grandfather of the legendary World War II general, George Patton, was mortally wounded.

Thousands of Confederates streamed through the city in retreat.

*   *   *

The Union cavalry had collapsed the left flank of the Confederate army. Early rushed to Brig. Gen. Bryan Grimes, who had taken over for Rodes, and ordered him to refuse the flank of his division to stave off the assault. With Grimes threatening to "blow the brains out" of any who broke for the rear, the Confederates tried to fashion

" . . . NOW OUR

DISASTERS

COMMENCED."

— CONFEDERATE

OFFICER

Confederates retreated pell-mell through Winchester. (wrhs)

a resistance. Grimes admitted in a letter home that the "troops did not behave with their usual valor." A foot soldier was in agreement when he wrote, "We had one of the worst stampedes from Winchester you ever heard of."

The confused retreat mixed commands, yet luckily for the Confederates, Ramseur's division kept its composure. The North Carolinian, who had opened the battle that morning, conducted a measured withdrawal and covered the retreat of the army as they fled from the field. This rearguard saved the majority of the wagons and artillery.

As the artillery was coming off the field, a comical occurrence happened between an artillerist and the Confederate army commander. As Pvt. Milton Humphrey's crew withdrew their artillery piece, Old Jube came upon them. Seeing they were trying to ram free the choked barrel, he ordered them to desist and leave the gun. One of the gun crew did not recognize the Confederate leader and exclaimed "go to Hell you damned old clodhopper and tend to your own business."

The "old clodhopper" did make one important decision that saved his army during the retreat. Colonel Thomas Munford's cavalry brigade was ordered from the far right to the collapsed left of the line. The Virginians that comprised the brigade arrived in Star Fort in time for artillery to be dragged out, saving valuable time for the hurriedly retreating Confederates.

Darkness finally enveloped the Valley. During the night, the Confederates continued to file down the Valley Turnpike. The bleak day witnessed the first time that Jackson's old Second Corps had ever been driven from a battlefield in the Shenandoah Valley.

The third—and what would be the final—battle of Winchester was over. For Sheridan, it had been a hard-won fight. There was little time to rest, though, for Little Phil's blood was up. He was not going to allow Early time to recover. The hounds were after the fox. At his headquarters

Fort Collier was built in July 1861 to guard the Valley Pike as it entered Winchester from the north. During the fighting of Third Winchester, Confederate artillerymen and soldiers— including men from the brigade of Col. George Patton— unsuccessfully defended Fort Collier against Union assaults. Today, earthworks are still present, and one can walk the grounds during daylight hours. The site is preserved by the Fort Collier Civil War Center, a non-profit organization dedicated to the preservations of the earthworks at Fort Collier. (dd/pg))

that night, the Federal commander issued orders for a pursuing march to begin at 5 a.m. the next morning.

In town, Winchester residents, unbeknown at the time, had seen the last of the Confederate army for the duration of the war. Winchester had changed hands for the last time.

Fisher's Hill

CHAPTER SIX

SEPTEMBER 19-22, 1864

The black night enveloped Jubal Early and his army as they marched south, away from the battlefield at Winchester. The Confederates were bound for Fisher's Hill, a prominence south of Strasburg that rose up from the Valley floor like a beacon to the retreating Confederates. As they marched south, spirits were mixed. One soldier remarked the army "was much jaded but not at all dispirited."

"Jaded"—and thinned in numbers. All told, Early had lost around 30 percent of his army at Third Winchester. The losses in the officer corps would have the most impact. The names of Robert Johnston, Archibald Godwin, George Patton, Fitz Lee, and Zebulon York could be found on the casualty list. Most damaging to the army was the death of Robert Rodes. In addition to these high level officers, more than 20 regimental commanders were lost.

Early wrote later that he halted at Fisher's Hill because "this was the only position in the whole Valley where a defensive line could be taken against an enemy moving up the Valley." Situated between Massanutten Mountain on the east and Little North Mountain on the west, this high ground was an ideal place for Early to consolidate his army. However, the position also had its weaknesses. The most glaring was that Early's infantry could not cover the entire line. Consequently, Early was forced to place cavalry on his left flank. Although it initially fought well at Third Winchester, the cavalry had become overmatched by their Union counterparts late on the day of September 19. Outnumbered and outgunned, the cavalry had lost control of the left flank

The American Battlefield Trust maintains a walking trail along Ramseur's position at Fisher's Hill. (cm)

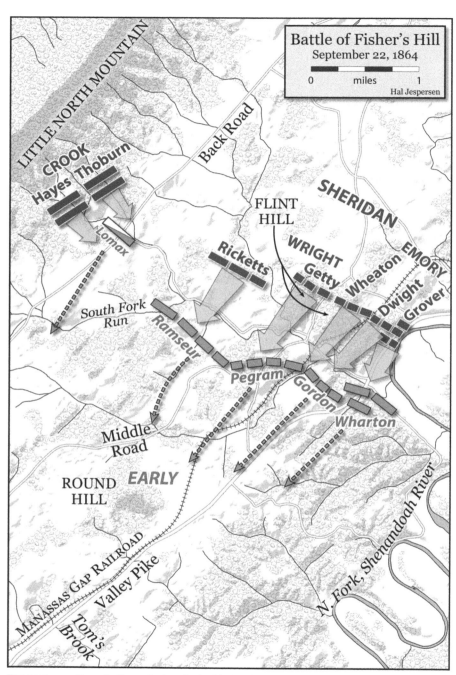

THE BATTLE OF FISHER'S HILL—Just as he had helped turn the tide at Third Winchester, George Crook played an important part in the battle of Fisher's Hill. Late in the afternoon, Crook attacked the Confederate flank. This poorly defended section quickly gave, allowing Crook to drive down the length of the Rebel line. Pressed by Crook on his left and Wright and Emory on his front, Early was forced to abandon Fisher's Hill.

which was one of the major reasons the Confederate line collapsed. Old Jube and the infantry had justifiable concern about the ability and morale of the cavaliers following Third Winchester.

The Union soldiers who marched south on the morning of September 20 were buoyed by the previous day's combat. A VI Corps surgeon wrote that Third Winchester was a "signal rout of the enemy and success to our arms."

While in pursuit of their prey, the Yankees no doubt took stock of their losses. They had lost between 4,000 and 5,000 men during the previous day's battle. Not the least of these was David Russell. His successor, Emory Upton, fell, too—wounded during the assault that broke the Rebel line. Also wounded and out of action was one of Crook's division commanders, Isaac Duval.

The Federal vanguard reached Strasburg in the afternoon and was greeted by an awesome sight. There before them lay the Army of the Valley, nestled in their fortifications atop Fisher's Hill. It was readily apparent, even to an aggressive officer like Sheridan, that any frontal assault would be suicidal. To discuss his options for an offensive, Little Phil called a council of war.

Sheridan received news of the rout at Winchester and immediately began plotting his move toward the Confederate position along Fisher's Hill. (loc)

Attending the conference were Crook, Emory, and Wright. The possibility of storming the position head on was quickly nixed. Moving around the enemy right, meanwhile, would expose the attackers to the signal station atop Massanutten Mountain and spoil the element of surprise. Crook suggested an attack on the left flank, situated near Little North Mountain. All things considered, this proposal was the most feasible, and Little Phil agreed. The Buzzards would attack the Confederate flank, and while they did, Alfred Torbert was ordered to take his horsemen and proceed through the adjoining Luray Valley to New Market Gap. It was Sheridan's hope that if the assault on Fisher's Hill was successful, then his horsemen would be able to cut off and trap the Army of the Valley as they retreated southward.

A postwar view of Fisher's Hill (loc)

Along Fisher's Hill, Early positioned his men from right to left in the following order. Gabriel Wharton's division held the extreme right near Massanutten Mountain. With a bend of the North Fork of the Shenandoah River, this position was almost unassailable. Lining up to the left of Wharton's division was John Gordon's veterans followed by Stephen Ramseur's division, now under the command of Brig. Gen. John Pegram. Ramseur slid over to take command of Rodes' division. He was a familiar face to the men in the ranks and had been personally requested to take command by a member of Rodes' staff.

On the left of Ramseur's division and holding the army's flank was the cavalry division of Maj. Gen. Lunsford L. Lomax. Compared to their Union counterparts, these horsemen were poorly armed and vastly undermanned. Veterans of the Army of the Valley questioned why these troopers were placed in this key defensive position. "All our misfortunes were caused by depending on the cavalry, a soldier in the 4th Georgia later wrote. "Neither fights [Third Winchester and Fisher's Hill] was our infantry whipped but forced to fall back because the cavalry let the Yankees flank our position."

Early never gave a reason why he overlooked his suspect alignment, writing only that "the enemy's immense superiority in cavalry and the inefficiency of the greater part of mine has been the cause of all my defeats." Historians have been left to marvel, without any definitive evidence because of the scarcity of Confederate primary accounts, why the cavalry were put in this vulnerable position.

Throughout September 21, the Federals shuffled their lines. In an effort to mask his movements, Sheridan extended the VI and XIX Corps beyond Strasburg. Meanwhile, the Army of West Virginia rested in the woods north of Cedar Creek. Another storm was approaching and the men knew it. On the morrow, it would start in earnest.

*   *   *

On September 22, Crook's Buzzards lived up to their other nickname, the "Mountain Creepers." That morning, the West Virginians marched around the rear of the army and, by noon, were poised to begin their final creep along the mountain. Around 2 p.m., their actual flanking maneuver commenced. "I formed my command in two columns," Crook wrote, "and marched them by the right flank along the side of the mountain."

Atop Fisher's Hill, Early had begun preparations to abandon the line. He ordered up the artillery caissons and chests to carry the ammunition so the withdrawal from the position at Fisher's Hill further up the Valley could begin quickly once darkness fell. Early knew an attack was imminent. Even holding such a strong position, Old Jube's thinned ranks could not withstand a wholesale onslaught.

Looking out from the
Confederate position atop
Ramseur's Hill toward
the Federal approach (dd/pg)

About a half mile from the enemy left, Crook deployed his men from column into line of battle. Around 4 p.m. with a shout, the Buzzards advanced down the mountain slope. The ground was so broken with rocks, thickets, and underbrush that all semblance of a formation was lost by the time the Federals struck the Confederate cavalry.

The assault did not come as a complete surprise. One Confederate artillerist spotted the Mountain Creepers "plainly climbing up the side of North Mountain." He added, "Gen. Early knows this and has troops there to meet them, and unless he has, we will have to get from this position, and very quickly."

The Union infantry slammed into the Confederate cavalry, and the left flank crumbled—overwhelmed by the ferocity of the Union attack, whose infantry were "yelling like madmen." Union Gen. Rutherford Hayes, in charge of a division, wrote afterwards that Confederate captives complained of being "thunderstruck" and "swore we had crossed the mountains." A Confederate infantryman wrote later that "our cavalry rushed down like the swine with an overdose of devils."

The 1st Maryland Cavalry (Confederate) attempted a counterattack to stem Crook's advance but was easily repulsed.

After brushing aside the cavalry, the divisions of Hays and Thoburn continued on toward the main Rebel battle line. Thoburn wrote afterwards that his men were "one large body of advancing soldiers, the bolder and stouter men being nearer the front, and the rear pushing eagerly forward and shouting and hurrahing and firing after the fast receding foe." Crook, meanwhile, remained behind the lines, a bundle of rocks under one arm, which he hurled at any of his men who tried to leave the ranks.

Witnessing the collapse of the cavalry, Stephen Ramseur repositioned Cullen Battle's Alabama brigade

Brig. Gen. George Crook had
already come to grief in the
Valley earlier in the year—
in July at the second battle
of Kernstown. By autumn,
he was ready for payback.
His men played critical roles in
the battles of Third Winchester
and Fisher's Hill. (loc)

Crook's "Mountain Creepers" formed up for their attack in these woods. (dd/pg)

and some artillery to meet the tidal wave of blue coming from the left flank. Ramseur also sent the brigade of William Cox to Battle's assistance. With all the confusion and scrambling, Cox got lost and did not participate in the fight. Battle's men, along with units from Bryan Grimes' brigade, did all they could to hold on. It would be for naught. As Crook's assault hit home, Horatio Wright ordered his VI Corps divisions forward. Struck in the front and flank, the Confederate line began to give way.

The VI Corps advanced from the heights opposite the Confederate position, crossed a stream known as Tumbling Run, and began their ascent of Fisher's Hill. James Ricketts' division overwhelmed the rest of Ramseur's division still posted in the main line. Early, arriving on the scene, ordered Gabriel Wharton to pull his division from the right of the line to reinforce the left.

Brig. Gen. Bryan Grimes, in charge of a brigade of North Carolinians, tried to maintain their defensive position even as the Confederate left flank collapsed. However, when the VI Corps launched a frontal assault against their position, the Confederates, faced with overwhelming numbers on two sides, began to give way. (loc)

This effort would be too little too late. As Hayes and Thoburn continued the attack, George Getty's division struck John Pegram, and Pegram's line also gave way. Pegram's retreat left only John Gordon's division in the main line. Gordon's ranks had been seriously thinned fighting for the Second Woods at Winchester, so it was not long before his ranks gave way before the pressure of Frank Wheaton's advance. Over on the right, soldiers from the XIX Corps occupied the enemy works that had been vacated by Gabriel Wharton.

Fisher's Hill now belonged to Sheridan's victorious legions.

The retreating Rebels streamed up the Valley Pike. Similar to Winchester, a few units maintained their integrity. A few officers were able to rally some soldiers near Mount Pleasant to further strengthen the Confederate rearguard.

As darkness blanketed the Valley, a firefight broke

out with some pursuing Yankees. One of the casualties of the skirmish was Alexander "Sandie" Pendleton. Now a lieutenant colonel, Pendleton had served faithfully on "Stonewall" Jackson's staff in the early stages of the war. After Jackson's death the previous spring, Pendleton remained with the Second Corps and was serving as Early's chief of staff. Shot in the abdomen, Pendleton died the next day in Woodstock. Early, in his memoirs of the last year of the war, said Pendleton "was acting with his accustomed gallantry" when he fell, "and his loss was deeply felt and regretted." From an irascible man like Early, this was high praise.

Although Early would write later that "our loss in killed and wounded in this affair was slight," he did admit that "some prisoners were taken." However, these simple statements do not attest to the damage to morale the army had suffered. For the second time in three days, Early's army had been put to flight. Coupled with the numbers lost in battle, morale plummeted.

During the retreat from Fisher's Hill, a Confederate infantryman remembered passing by a comrade who was casually cooking his supper near the road. The man could be heard singing an impromptu song. One of the lines: "Old Jube Early's about played out."

The Federals attacked uphill toward Confederates positioned along the crest. (dd/pg)

Laying Waste to the Valley

CHAPTER SEVEN
SEPTEMBER 22-OCTOBER 5, 1864

The Federal pursuit continued through the night of September 22 and reached the village of Woodstock the next day. When Little Phil rode into town that morning, he hoped that his victory would be complete. Unfortunately, he learned that Alfred Torbert's foray into the Luray Valley had been turned back by Confederate cavalry under Col. Thomas Munford and Brig. Gen. Williams C. Wickham.

On the following day, September 24, Sheridan vented his anger toward his mounted arm by relieving William Averell from command for failing to follow up the pursuit of the shattered Confederates. Sheridan had given Averell strict orders to follow them and engage, and although Averell had complied, he failed to give battle on a scale to Little Phil's liking. Sheridan replaced him with Col. William Powell.

Regardless of who was to blame, the complete destruction of Jubal Early's army would have to wait for another day.

With the Federals arriving in Woodstock, Early's army continued its retreat to Mount Jackson, more than 23 miles south of the Fisher's Hill battlefield. There, Early called a halt to "enable the sick and wounded, and the hospital stores at that place to be carried off." Afterwards, the retreat of the Southerners continued to Rude's Hill between Mount Jackson and New Market.

Early might have recounted nonchalantly the Confederate retreat in his reporting and later writings, but the twin defeats at Third Winchester and Fisher's Hill had shocked the rank and file. Since many had served under Stonewall Jackson, the soldiers lamented

Early held this area on Rude's Hill following his defeat at Fisher's Hill (left). Roadside markers along the Valley Turnpike, including this one erected by the United Daughters of the Confederacy (above), discuss the location's importance during the war. (cm)

Crook's men marched through downtown Harrisonburg. (wrhs)

Residents in New Market felt the waves of war wash back and forth through the village. (cm)

the difference between campaigns in the Shenandoah Valley. "Oh what a difference between Jackson's army and the fire he put into us and the will to fight and how it all dried up under Early," one of them bemoaned. Another soldier, writing after Third Winchester, put it more plainly: "What was left of our army now lost all confidence in General Early as a leader, and they were therefore much demoralized."

On September 24, the Army of the Shenandoah marched south in pursuit. Considering the bedraggled condition of the Army of the Valley, Early smartly withdrew, marching through New Market and on to Port Republic. The battered Confederates did not stop until they reached Brown's Gap in the Blue Ridge Mountains.

Sheridan followed, finally halting in Harrisonburg, a little more than 70 miles from Winchester. After setting up headquarters, Little Phil reviewed the previous week's fighting and pondered his future plans. The Army of the Shenandoah had suffered about 700 casualties at Fisher's Hill, comparatively less than at Third Winchester. Despite this, Sheridan elected not to march on Brown's Gap.

This decision undoubtedly caused Ulysses S. Grant some consternation. Exchanging messages with his Valley commander, Grant urged—then pleaded with—Sheridan to move east, crush Early, and capture Charlottesville. Such a movement would leave the infrastructure of central Virginia vulnerable to the Federals. In Grant's mind, this undertaking and any subsequent operations would help bring about the fall of Richmond and Petersburg. Grant insisted that the Confederates were reeling from Sheridan's recent victories, which were, in Grant's words, "causing great consternation."

Sheridan balked at his commander's ideas, contenting himself with remaining in Harrisonburg. He felt it would be difficult for his army to subsist on what it could forage while marching through Virginia's interior. Writing later, Sheridan insisted that if he encountered strong resistance during such a movement, "a lack of supplies might compel me to abandon the attempt." Rather than wreaking a path of destruction through the Commonwealth, he would concentrate on his immediate vicinity.

When Sheridan had received command in August, Grant's instructions were quite clear: "eat out Virginia clean and clear . . . so that a crow flying over it will have to carry their own provender." Additionally, Sheridan was directed to "do all the damage to railroads . . . carry off stock of all descriptions" and, "if the war is to last another year, we want the Shenandoah Valley to remain a barren waste." In the spirit of these orders, Sheridan directed his men to visit fire and brimstone on the local landscape for the next 10 days. Anything of subsistence, including crops and hay, was burned. Livestock was slaughtered. From Staunton to Port Republic and on to Waynesboro, nothing was left to supply Early or Gen. Robert E. Lee.

One of the best sources about the extent of the destruction in the Valley comes from Rockingham County, which has its county seat at Harrisonburg and ranks as one of the largest counties in Virginia. After the Union soldiers departed, the officers of the county court organized a committee to assess the damages. The final list was published in the *Register and Advertiser* of Rockingham County. Not taking into account personal belongings or miscellaneous outbuildings, the effectiveness of the destruction is chilling. The committee found 30 dwelling houses burned; 450 barns burned; 100 miles of fencing destroyed; and 31 mills, 3 factories, and 1 furnace burned.

The Harrisonburg town square as it appeared when Sheridan's army occupied the area (wrhs)

As the Confederacy's breadbasket, the Shenandoah finally saw the hard hand of war under Sheridan. Here is a modern view of an area outside Harrisonburg that suffered under "the burning." (dd/pg)

In addition, 1,750 cattle, 1,750 horses, 4,200 sheep, and 3,350 hogs had been carried off; and 100,000 bushels of wheat, 50,000 bushels of corn, and 6,332 tons of hay had been destroyed.

A Mennonite resident of the Valley, surveying the destruction around his family farm, wrote:

> *The Union army came up the Valley sweeping everything before them like a hurricane; there was nothing left for man or beast from the horse down to the chicken; all was taken. So we felt as though we could not subsist; and besides, they were burning down barns and mills in every direction around us.*

As part of a religious sect that adhered to a decree of nonaggression, the man made a decision to get a pass from the Union army and head north out of harm's way.

The destruction seemed to instill a sense of retribution and resolve in the Confederate ranks. "Our hearts ached at the horrible sight," one soldier recounted, "our beautiful Valley almost a barren waste and we with an army so inferior in numbers as to render success almost hopeless. Yet the sight carried with it unseen power . . . to avenge this dastardly warfare, making us doubly equal to such an enemy."

Lt. John Meigs was killed in a skirmish with Confederate cavalry outside Dayton. (wrhs)

The loss to the Confederacy's war effort was irreparable, though. Lee's army, fighting from the siege lines of Richmond and Petersburg, depended on supplies from the Shenandoah Valley to survive. With such devastation, many a soldier, along with many a civilian on the home front, faced a bleak and hungry winter.

*   *   *

On October 3, while overseeing a survey, one of Sheridan's staff officers, Lt. John Meigs, encountered several Confederate cavalrymen. In the skirmish that ensued, Meigs was killed (see Tour #4). Besides being an engineer on Sheridan's staff, he was also the son of the quartermaster general of the United States Army, Montgomery Meigs. Sheridan was livid when he received word of the young man's death. In an act of vengeance, he ordered all the houses in the area near the skirmish burned along with the entire town of Dayton. Fortunately for the local citizens, Col. Thomas Wildes of the 116th Ohio requested that Sheridan rescind the order. In an uncharacteristic action, Little Phil acquiesced, thus saving the town.

A plaque in Dayton honors Col. Thomas Wildes' refusal to torch the town. The plaque is located at the intersection of Main Street and Mill Street. (dd/pg)

The Confederates needed a response to the Federal destruction. Despite the low morale and continued disparity in numbers, there was one characteristic about Early no one could deny. A Confederate soldier put it succinctly: "What ever may have been Earlys' faults, he was a fighter."

Two days after Meigs' death, the Army of the Shenandoah withdrew from Harrisonburg, marching north down the Valley. As the Northerners began their trek back down the Valley, they began to see Southern horsemen on the distant horizon, creeping ever closer. Another fight was brewing.

Tom's Brook

CHAPTER EIGHT

OCTOBER 5-9, 1864

On October 5, the Federals began their march down the Valley, with infantry and supply wagons marching down the Valley Pike. Wesley Merritt's division marched along the turnpike, too, as well as along a parallel thoroughfare known as the Middle Road. James Wilson's division, now under the command of Brig. Gen. George A. Custer, marched along the Back Road.

Custer had ascended to command on September 30 when Wilson was transferred back to the Western Theatre to take command of the Cavalry Corps of the Military Division of the Mississippi. In the closing days of the war, Wilson would distinguish himself leading a massive cavalry raid into the Deep South. Wilson's new assignment may have been the result of standing in high favor with Grant: Wilson had served on Grant's staff throughout 1863 and into early 1864. Custer's resulting elevation was the product of his own tenacious fighting. The young brigadier had distinguished himself during the Gettysburg and Overland campaigns.

After hearing of the defeats at Third Winchester and Fisher's Hill, Gen. Robert E. Lee decided to send reinforcements to Early. Serving in the Valley during the early stages of the campaign, Maj. Gen. Joseph Kershaw's infantry division and Maj. Wilfred Cutshaw's artillery battalion, consisting of 12 guns, began their return trip on September 23. Kershaw could count around 2,500 muskets to add to Early's strength.

In addition to these forces, Lee also dispatched the 600-man "Laurel Brigade." Known for wearing badges made of laurel leaves, the unit consisted of three regiments and a battalion of Virginia cavalry. Its commander was a veteran cavalier, Brig. Gen. Thomas Rosser. Shortly after his arrival, Rosser would be given the nickname "Savior of the Valley"—a play to the trust

From the parking lot of St. Matthew's Lutheran Church, one can see the hilltop where Confederate cavalry encamped. Tom's Brook runs along the base of the wooded hill. (cm)

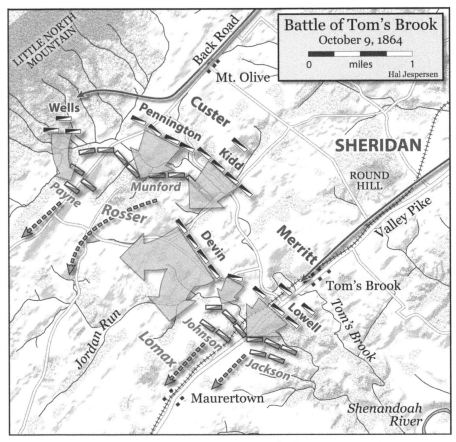

THE BATTLE OF TOM'S BROOK—Munford was in command on Spiker's Hill early in the engagement. Two of the three regiments in Custer's attack belonged to Wells' brigade. Payne attacked across the hill late in the battle but was caught in the flank attack.

and bravado that Rosser bestowed upon himself and the Laurel Brigade. There is some ambiguity as to who christened him with the term and whether it was made seriously or in jest. Rosser would not be in command of the unit long, though. He would take over Brig. Gen. Williams C. Wickham's division when Wickham left to take a seat in the Confederate Congress. Lieutenant Colonel Richard Dulany would then be promoted to command Rosser's cavalry.

Early's other cavalry division, headed by Lunsford Lomax, could only count some 800 men to fill its ranks.

As the days grew darker at Richmond and Petersburg, Lee's commitment of these additional troops underscored his intentions. After the fall of Atlanta and with the presidential election looming, salvaging the hopes of an independent Confederacy rested in the Shenandoah Valley.

Custer oversaw some of the destruction wrought on crops as the army moved northward. (loc)

With a renewed purpose, Early set off in pursuit of Sheridan.

*   *   *

As the Yankees marched north, the cavalry continued the destruction begun around Harrisonburg. "As we marched along," Sheridan wrote, "the many columns of smoke from burning stacks and mills filled with grain indicated that the . . . country was . . . losing its features which . . . had made it a great magazine of stores for the Confederate armies."

Rosser's division followed Custer along the Back Road while Lomax rode after Merritt. The damage wrought by the Federals infuriated the Confederate cavalry. Many of the troopers, including Rosser's old Laurel Brigade, hailed from the Valley. As a result, the fighting with the Federals intensified. James Taylor, an illustrator for *Frank Leslie's Illustrated Newspaper*, recalled the action on Custer's front. "The rear guard followed at a slow walk," he wrote. "When the enemy pressed too close, the men would halt and face about, a brisk fusillade would last a few moments, when the graycoats would be off . . . the rear guard would halt at the edge of the next hill or belt of woods to repeat the operation."

By the evening of October 8, Custer had reached a point just north of Mount Olive Church. Rosser's men were just a few miles south, atop an eminence known as Spiker's Hill. Below Spiker's Hill ran a stream called Tom's Brook. The name also lent itself to a hamlet nearby. Merritt's division went into camp at the base of another elevation known as Round Hill. Lomax occupied high ground south of another stream called Jordan Run.

That night, Sheridan called his cavalry chief, Alfred Torbert, to his headquarters. Livid with the audacity of

Looking toward Sheridan's headquarters from Lomax's position (dd/pg)

the Confederates and their harassment of his cavalry, Sheridan ordered Torbert to set out the next morning and give battle to the enemy.

*   *   *

Dawn came with a hint of snow in the air. At 6:30 a.m., Wesley Merritt began his march toward Lomax's position. Leading Merritt's division was Col. Charles R. Lowell's brigade. Lowell was to move forward and meet the Confederates along the Valley Pike, while Col. Thomas Devin's brigade flanked the Confederate line west of the road.

Lomax had two brigades drawn up in battle formation, Col. Bradley Johnson's to the left of the Pike and Lt. Col. William Thompson's to the right. When Lowell's men came in sight, Lomax ordered Thompson forward. In reality, there was little Lomax could do. In fact, the men under Lomax would be termed by a Confederate officer from the inspector general's office as "very poorly armed" and "cannot be properly termed Cavalry."

Brig. Gen. Wesley Merritt's troopers fought Confederate cavalry along the Valley Turnpike during the battle of Tom's Brook. (loc)

Lowell and his New Englanders successfully parried Thompson's blows and drove the Rebels back. Lowell then prepared for a counterattack. With Devin's troopers advancing on his flank and Lowell moving on his front, Lomax was forced to abandon his position. Lomax was able to hold off Merritt's men until they reached the countryside south of the town of Woodstock. There, facing overwhelming numbers, the Confederate withdrawal escalated into a rout. Terror gripped the Rebels, and Merritt's division chased them down the pike.

Meanwhile, Merritt's last brigade, under Col. James Kidd, was maneuvering through the countryside between the turnpike and the Back Road. Just several days earlier, these men had been commanded by George Custer. Their former brigadier was having a tough go of it that morning, and the brigade was on its way to his assistance.

Custer's division had marched out of camp early that morning heading toward Mount Olive. There, his leading brigade under Col. Alexander Pennington ran into Rosser's pickets. Pennington's men quickly gained the upper hand and pushed the Rebels to their main line. With Custer's men coming into view from Spiker's Hill, word went back to Rosser's headquarters about the advance. Arriving on the field, Rosser joined the brigade of Thomas Munford, who was already in position along the hill where the Back Road crossed the stream. Rosser deployed William Payne's brigade on Munford's right with the Laurel Brigade on Payne's right.

As Custer and his staff crested a ridge, they came in view of the Rebel lines. Scanning Spiker's Hill, Custer recognized his old West Point chum Rosser. Riding ahead of his staff, Custer removed his hat and bowed to his friend. Rosser returned the pleasantry. Custer then called out, "Let us have a fair fight and no malice." Both sides erupted in cheers.

Rosser held a strong position atop Spiker's Hill. Rather than commit to an all-out assault, Custer decided to probe the position with Pennington's men. He would keep his other brigade, under Col. William Wells, in reserve. Pennington's troopers charged down the hill and across the stream. The Yankees ran into stiff resistance

A view of the Confederate position from Custer's lines (dd/pg)

Col. Thomas Devin had earned a reputation as "a hard hitter" during his service under the late Brig. Gen. John Buford earlier in the war. (loc)

Custer saluted his old chum Rosser with a sweep of his hat, then called for "a fair fight and no malice." (loc)

Brig. Gen. Thomas Rosser's troopers harassed Custer's men as they withdrew from Harrisonburg. (moc)

from the Laurel Brigade and were driven back across Tom's Brook. Near the road crossing, another thrust was driven back by Munford's brigade. With his initial assaults stymied, Custer was forced to cast about for other options if he hoped to win the day.

The alternative appeared in the form of Kidd's brigade. With a firm grip on Rosser's line at Spiker's Hill, Custer decided to use his old command to assail the Confederate right. As Kidd's men moved forward, Custer decided to send three regiments to attack from the west. The assault could not have been coordinated better. Custer linked up with Kidd and quickly began to drive in the Confederate position. The three regiments surprised the Rebels and caved in Rosser's flank. The Confederates tried to stem the tide, but it was no use. As one soldier recounted, "Every soldier knows that it only requires a shout in the rear to keep a stampeded force on the run, and it was so now." As the participant noted, Rosser's line disintegrated.

Years later, Munford would remark that the engagement at Tom's Brook "became more a contest of speed than valor." As the Confederates fled the field, attempts were made to rally them. However, the retreat would become a race to reach the safety of the Confederate infantry. All told, the Union cavalry would chase the Rebels more than 20 miles—all the way to Columbia Furnace—scooping up prisoners as well as wagons and artillery along the way. Merritt did not let up until he reached Jubal Early's infantry at Rude's Hill.

Forever after, Tom's Brook would be known amongst the Union cavalry as "Woodstock Races."

Rosser attacked Custer along the Back Road. (loc)

Old Jube always had misgivings about his cavalry. From the beginning of the campaign, he had viewed his cavalry with suspicion and often used the infantry to undertake reconnaissances, such as the one that almost doomed the army prior to Third Winchester. His view of his cavalry's effectiveness waned even further after their poor showing at Fisher's Hill, even though they were put at a disadvantage on the extreme left of the Confederate army. The bravado that Rosser showed when he assumed command rankled Early, who later complained of Rosser's "ridiculous vaporing." When Rosser went further, suggesting that the Laurel Brigade would "show the rest of [Early's] command how to fight," it completely turned Early sour toward the younger Virginian. The affair at Tom's Brook only added to Early's disgust.

He still held faith in his infantry, though. Despite the fact that his ranks were depleted, Early, always the fighter, felt there was still an opportunity to tip the scales in his favor. The time and place to give battle would have to be near perfect to neutralize the numerical superiority of the enemy. In choosing the location to fight, Early would attempt to invoke the memory of Stonewall Jackson. Like a boxer staggering from a few body blows, he would sum up the strength for one last counterpunch. With thoughts of an offensive on his mind, the Confederates resumed their hunt for Sheridan.

Preparations for Battle

CHAPTER NINE
OCTOBER 10-18, 1864

The resounding victory of October 9, 1864, was further proof to Phil Sheridan that the Rebels were finished. In his mind, he had whipped the Confederates at Third Winchester and Fisher's Hill. Now, he had soundly defeated the cavalry at Tom's Brook. Taken together with the thorough dismantling and destruction of the agricultural infrastructure, Sheridan believed that the campaign was effectively over—an opinion he'd come to back when his army encamped around Harrisonburg some two weeks ago. Two days after Tom's Brook, he had written to Grant of his thorough "cleaning out of the stock, forage, wheat, provisions, etc. in the Valley."

That is why, as he marched north from Strasburg on October 10, Sheridan ordered the VI Corps toward Front Royal while the rest of the army went into camp along Cedar Creek, just south of Middletown. It was Little Phil's intention that the VI Corps return to the front at Richmond and Petersburg.

When this intelligence reached Early, the Confederate commander moved to counteract this possibility. Lee's army, ensconced around Richmond and Petersburg, already faced overwhelming numbers. The return of the VI Corps would only add to the disparity. Early had figured out "what [Sheridan] intends doing" and laid out to Lee the options he had before him.

Early didn't wait for a response, though, and on October 12, the Confederate army began its march down the Valley.

"This is a time of great trial," wrote Maj. Gen. Stephen Ramseur to a family member, assuring the relative "we are all called on to show that we are made

A stone monument sits next to the Valley Turnpike near the Hupp's Hill Civil War Park. Interestingly, there is no inscription on the monument. While it stands near a historical marker citing the nearby entrenchments, the origins and the intent of the monument are unknown. (cm)

The Hupp's Hill Civil War Park offers a museum with exhibits that encompass the actions in the Valley in 1864 (above). Visitors can explore the property through walking trails that follow Civil War entrenchments (right). (cm)

of the true metal." Early would put that "true metal" to the test shortly.

Most of the army went into camp around Woodstock on the night of October 12. By the next day, Early's army had approached the vicinity of Fisher's Hill, the scene of their reversal the previous month. The next morning, October 13, the Army of the Valley suddenly appeared at Hupp's Hill, just south of Cedar Creek. Confederate artillery soon maneuvered into place, and the artillerists went through the procedures of ramming in a welcome message to their Union counterparts. The first shells arched through the sky and into the camp of the XIX Corps, scattering the blue-coated soldiers in every direction. In response, the Yankees sent the brigades of Col. George Wells and Col. Thomas Harris across the stream to investigate.

During the ensuing fight, the two sides slugged away at each other. Finally, the Confederates brought up reinforcements and managed to drive the Yankees back to their encampment.

Both sides had little to show for the skirmish, save for the loss of two brigade commanders. The wound sustained by Confederate Col. James Connor resulted in the amputation of a leg. Union Col. George D. Wells did not fare as well. He died from a chest wound. Ultimately, Early withdrew back to his old position at Fisher's Hill.

The skirmish was enough for Sheridan to countermarch the VI Corps to Middletown. Still, the Federal commander felt that the campaign and the part his army had played were over. Unfortunately for Sheridan, Grant did not agree. He continued to prod Sheridan to commence operations against the Virginia Central and Orange and Alexandria railroads in central Virginia. A three-day cavalry expedition did little to satisfy the commanding general.

Brig. Gen. James Conner was wounded at Hupp's Hill. (wrhs)

*   *   *

The day after Hupp's Hill, Sheridan received a telegram from Secretary of War Edwin Stanton. The secretary wanted to weigh in on the matter of future operations and wanted to speak to Sheridan first before consulting the general in chief. On the night of October 15, Sheridan began the trip to Washington, leaving his army in the hands of Maj. Gen. Horatio Wright. When Sheridan consented to a meeting in Washington with the top brass of the Union war effort, he was content that Confederates posed no offensive threat to his army.

The Confederates, however, declined to be quite so accommodating.

As if he needed any urging from Lee, Early was putting the initial plans in motion for an attack. He set on a flanking movement as the most likely to succeed. Lee believed that if Early could use his entire army "it [victory] can be accomplished." That was all the direction the ever-aggressive Early needed to advance his plans.

On October 17, Early directed Maj. Gen. John Gordon; Brig. Gen. Clement Evans, who commanded a brigade under Gordon; and Jedediah Hotchkiss, the

Col. George D. Wells, brevetted brigadier general, was mortally wounded during the action at Hupp's Hill on October 13, 1864. His bust sits atop a monument in the Winchester National Cemetery. (dd/pg)

The village of Middletown. Sheridan's army encamped in the surrounding area after the battle of Tom's Brook. (wrhs)

Gordon and Hotchkiss undertook a reconnaissance mission atop Massanutten Mountain to scope out Federal positions. (wrhs)

army's topographical engineer, to conduct a thorough examination of Sheridan's lines. Suffering from arthritis, Early was unable to scale the steep summit of Massanutten Mountain, known as the "Three Sisters."

Ever one for drama, Gordon wrote later that their view of the Union lines "was an inspiring panorama." What was visible to Gordon was "not only the general outlines of Sheridan's breastworks, but every parapet where his heavy guns were mounted, and every piece of artillery." Furthermore, Gordon boasted that he could see "distinctly the three colors of trimmings on the jackets respectively of infantry, artillery, and cavalry, and locate each, while the number of flags gave a basis for estimating approximately the forces we were to contend with." This opportunity, reminisced Gordon, "required . . . no transcendent military genius to decide" on the course of action the Confederates could take.

A view of Massanutten Mountain from the rear of the Union lines at Cedar Creek (dd/pg)

Hotchkiss went to work doing what he did best, making a map of the Union positions and the topography. As the trio returned that night, they hammered out a plan, and Hotchkiss left to report the findings to Early.

* * *

The next day, Early was approached by another of his division commanders, Brig. Gen. John Pegram, who had devised a plan of his own. Hotchkiss was present when Pegram outlined his thoughts, and the cartographer proceeded to report what his party had perceived and strategized the night before. Early was noncommittal and sent out a request to his subordinates to report to headquarters and discuss future operations.

The four other infantry division commanders—Gordon, Ramseur, Kershaw, and Wharton—joined Pegram in answer to Early's summons. Also in attendance were Thomas Rosser and artillery chief Col. Thomas Carter.

The meeting convened around 2 p.m. Gordon did most of the talking. The plan he and Hotchkiss outlined was a flanking movement by the Second Corps around the Union left. This maneuver would be followed by a determined frontal assault by the rest of the army.

A question arose concerning the viability of marching an entire corps across the north face of Massanutten Mountain and across the North Fork of the Shenandoah River, which flowed along the base of the prominence. Gordon, who was as persistent as they came when he had his mind made up, insisted that a route could be found and that the enemy would believe the feat impracticable, thus ensuring the chance of a surprise assault. In the end, Gordon swayed the officers present, including Early, by stating he would accept full responsibility if the plan backfired. He would take 6,200 men of the Second Corps on a sweeping flank attack around the Union left—exactly the kind of maneuver these former men of Stonewall Jackson's were accustomed to.

The Georgian's plan won out and orders were issued to the different commands. Working in concert with the Second Corps' assignment, Kershaw's division would head to Bowman's Ford along Cedar Creek and cross there. Wharton and the artillery would be guided by the Valley Pike to Hupp's Hill; when he saw or heard that Gordon and Kershaw engaged, he was to pass down the Valley Pike and push to Middletown. Rosser's cavalry would cross Cedar Creek at Cupp's Mill Ford and initiate the engagement by taking on their Union counterparts. Other cavalry under Col. William Payne, who was also present at the headquarters meeting, would lead Gordon's advance, surprising any Union pickets along the way before making a dash toward Belle Grove, an impressive country home that was known to be the headquarters of Sheridan. Gordon's plan had Payne's Confederate cavalry making an attempt at capturing the Union commander.

All units were ordered to be in position by 5:00 a.m. In the words of Evans, who had been part of the triumvirate that ascended Massanutten Mountain on October 17, the chance presented to the Confederates held the possibility to "utterly rout them." That was the dream of Early and Gordon.

Cedar Creek, Part 1

CHAPTER TEN
OCTOBER 18-19, 1864

Early's greatest gamble of the campaign began under the cover of darkness.

Confederate soldiers began assembling and shuffling off to their assigned positions in the battle plan. One officer remembered the night as "cloudy and cold," which limited visibility, and the men "glided along the road like a procession of specters through the dark."

North of Cedar Creek, as the men of the Army of the Shenandoah bedded down, there was no indication that the next day would be any different than the last. Sheridan's soldiers had spent the last few days lounging about their camps reading mail and casting their ballots for the upcoming election.

The Federal line extended across the hills and ridges above Cedar Creek. The VI Corps held the right with the XIX Corps in the center, its left resting near the Valley Turnpike. George Crook's Buzzards and a provisional division commanded by Col. J. Howard Kitching occupied the left.

Gordon's men were in position sometime after 3 a.m. They were directed to rest until the attack order came. The other divisions had been filing into place at the same time, along with the cavalry. As the minutes ticked by, anxiety levels rose for the Southerners. Even Early felt anxious. "Colonel, this is the most trying experience of my life," he admitted to a staff officer; "if only I could pray like Stonewall Jackson."

* * *

Thomas Rosser's two brigades were in place and tasked with creating the diversionary attack to begin the

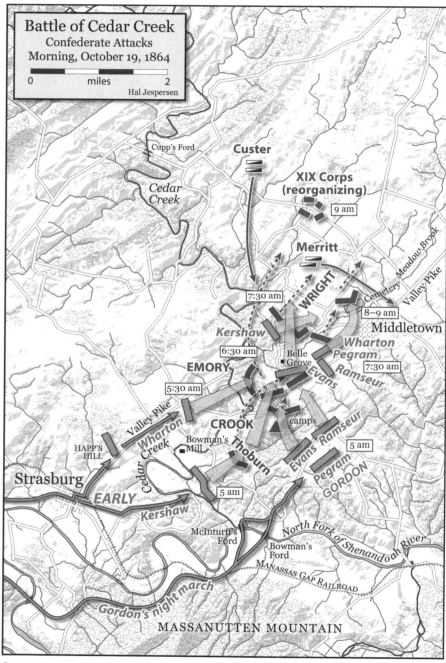

CONFEDERATE ATTACKS DURING THE BATTLE OF CEDAR CREEK—During the early morning hours of October 19, 1864, Confederates moved into position to attack the Union left flank. Kershaw's and Gordon's men quickly overran Crook's Army of West Virginia before crashing into Emory's XIX Corps. By mid-morning, Wright's VI Corps had been driven from their positions, as well, and the Confederates held the field.

Maj. Gen. Joseph Kershaw's 2,500 Confederates crossed at Bowman's Mill Ford to attack the Union lines. (dd/pg)

general offensive. The time was 4:30 a.m. when Col. Thomas Owen, leading the 3rd Virginia Cavalry, moved his men quietly toward the enemy. In addition, Col. William Payne's cavalry brigade would make a dash at the Union pickets, capture as many as they could, and advance toward Belle Grove in a desperate attempt to capture Sheridan.

Unable to stand the tension any longer, Joseph Kershaw's division moved forward when the noise generated by the cavalry of Payne's Brigade, which advanced in front of the Second Corps on the opposite flank, carried down to their position. Crossing at Bowman's Ford, Kershaw's division was spearheaded by Georgians, commanded this day by Col. James P. Simms. The rest of the division followed.

The 2nd Battalion of the 5th New York Heavy Artillery was posted along Crook's picket line near Bowman's Ford. All through the night, these artillerists-turned-infantrymen could hear strange noises coming from their front and across Cedar Creek. Suddenly, out of the early morning mist, charged Kershaw's Southerners. Taken by surprise, the Empire Staters fired a ragged volley and then ran for the rear, Kershaw's men hot on their heels. Simms' Georgians struck the Federal entrenchments near a gap between the brigades of Cols. Thomas Wildes and Thomas Harris. These brigades, belonging to Joseph Thoburn's division, were "subjected to enfilading fires . . . these two brigades were driven from the works . . . a large portion of the men flying . . . in great disorder."

With the Rebels pouring over the works, Thoburn's line was quickly overrun, exposing Capt. Henry DuPont's artillery. Visibility was limited, as DuPont recalled, "in consequence of the mist"—but he opened

The battle of Cedar Creek (loc)

fire nonetheless. Facing overwhelming numbers, the Delawarean's gunners held on in the hopes that they could slow the enemy advance long enough for troops from the XIX Corps to form. The resistless Confederate tide swept over the position, though, and the artillerists headed for the rear—losing only one piece in the process.

Gordon's corps was still resting south of the river at this time. It was 4:35 a.m. when Col. William Payne's cavalry trotted past the waiting infantry. Gordon then issued orders for the infantry to fall in. Shortly afterwards, the command "Forward" rang out, and the Confederate flanking assault began.

In columns of four came Gordon's infantry, protected behind their cavalry screen. The first men to bear the brunt of the surprise maneuver were the 34th Ohio Infantry, whose sleepy pickets along the river were quickly gobbled up. Confederates then felt the sting of the Shenandoah's icy water as they crossed the North Fork; one Georgian remembered the "scramble" of men that "took place to see who should get first across."

On the far side, Gordon's men arrived at the John Cooley farm and found themselves astride the flank of the Army of West Virginia. West of the farmstead, Gordon aligned his corps for the assault. His old division, commanded by Clement Evans, comprised his left flank. John Pegram deployed the two brigades in his division behind Evans. The right of the line was held by Maj. Gen. Stephen Ramseur's division. Minutes before the sun rose to usher in the day, Gordon's men went forward, seven abreast.

Coming out of the mist and fog of the early morning, Clement Evans drove his men toward Rutherford Hayes' division. The Rebels struck Hayes at an opportune time: only half of the division had been ordered into position; the rest remained in camp. As had happened in Thoburn's division, the Federal line disintegrated. Hayes' collapse left Kitching isolated. He

was quickly overrun by Ramseur's division, screaming the Rebel Yell.

In a span of some 30 minutes, the left flank of the Army of the Shenandoah was gone.

*   *   *

"It has always been somewhat of a mystery where Early obtained the troops with which he fought this battle," a befuddled Vermonter later said, summing up the effect of Early's morning assault. In actuality, Early's only infantry reinforcement had been Kershaw's division, but these Rebels made a difference on this October morning. Kershaw, along with Evans, drove onward. They continued toward the Valley Turnpike and Maj. Gen. William Emory's XIX Corps.

These Union veterans were under arms when the fighting started. In very quick succession, the sounds of battle crept closer to them. Emory's line faced south, and Emory knew it would take time to pull his men out of the earthworks and meet the threat bearing down from the east. This would be no easy task.

Coming from the southeast, the now-united Confederate advance had driven back one Union corps and now looked toward damaging another. However,

Belle Grove (above) still wears the scars of battle in its masonry and woodwork (below). (cm, dd/pg)

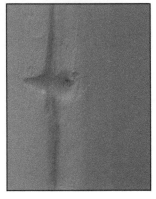

Near Belle Grove, looking south toward XIX Corps' line
(dd/pg)

something other than Union shot and shell would help delay the advance. In their morning assaults, the Southerners had overrun the Northern camps and uncovered a cornucopia of goods. One Confederate officer remarked that "the smoking breakfast, just ready for the table, stood temptingly inviting, while the opened tents displayed a scene almost enchanting to the eyes of the Southern soldier."

"Good gracious what a feast we had!" exclaimed

another officer as their battle line started leaking soldiers. Napoleon's comment, "An army moves on its stomach," was never more evident than at Cedar Creek. The fact that the soldiers of Early's army could not resist the temptation of the Union camps showed the effectiveness of "The Burning" Sheridan's army had undertaken in the Valley. It also illustrated the inability of the Confederacy at this stage of the war to properly equip and supply its fighting men.

Many of the Rebels were motivated more by their success than their stomachs, though, and the onslaught of Evans, Kershaw, Pegram, and Ramseur continued.

Emory ordered Brig. Gen. James McMillan to send a brigade toward the sound of the fighting in an effort to allow Emory to reform his men. McMillan decided to send his old brigade to a ridgeline east of the turnpike. Led by Col. Stephen Thomas, the 8th Vermont, 12th Connecticut, and 160th New York marched across the turnpike and took up a position on a wooded ridge. There, the Yankees met Gordon's screaming, onrushing ranks. The fighting that ensued was "a horrid, desperate, hand-to-hand encounter," one soldier shivered. Severely outnumbered, all three Federal regiments suffered heavy casualties.

Thomas' counterattack had the desired effect, though. It allowed Emory enough time to fashion a new line with his corps. His veterans put up a stubborn defense, but soon, even they were overwhelmed and were driven from their position, streaming westward across a tributary of Cedar Creek known as Meadow Brook.

In a little under two hours, two-thirds of the Army of the Shenandoah had dissolved under the waves of Stonewall's old command. Just like an apparition from the late Stonewall, the Confederates had appeared out of the fog and had struck the Union line hard.

Now, all that remained between the Confederates and complete victory was the Union VI Corps.

The 8th Vermont lost 106 of 175 men they engaged in their counterattack against the Confederates. A monument to the regiment is located southeast of the Belle Grove driveway. Because of the undulating nature of the land, though, it cannot be seen from the Valley Turnpike. (dd/pg)

The 128th New York fought valiantly, but the gray onslaught overwhelmed them. A monument remembering their action sits near the XIX Corps entrenchments, just to the west of the Valley Turnpike. (dd/pg)

Cedar Creek,
Part II

CHAPTER ELEVEN
OCTOBER 19, 1864

As Jubal Early crossed over Cedar Creek, he rode through the captured Union camps and saw his army gathering much-needed supplies. As hungry as the men might be, though, now was not the time. Early sent his staff officers to stop the soldiers from looting the camps and "orders were sent to the division commanders to send for their men."

The day had been a success so far. The cantankerous Early had seen his army overrun two Union positions. He needed only to finish the rout.

As the Confederate commander approached the front line, he ran into Gordon, who briefed him on the situation. The Georgian had just sent the divisions of Kershaw and Evans toward the Union VI Corps camps. Ramseur and Pegram had come to a rest on the Valley Turnpike north of where the two officers met. Gabriel Wharton's infantry division was also arriving on the field. Along with artillery battalions commanded by Thomas Carter, these troops could help in the Confederate offensive against the VI Corps.

However, the early morning fog that had shielded the initial Confederate approach now mixed with the smoke to obscure the troop positions Gordon summarized. In addition, the fog obscured how soundly the Confederates had pushed the enemy from the field and the rout that had consumed these Union soldiers.

Literally, the fog of war had settled over the battlefield—over the armies, over Gordon, over Early—as their later accounts would testify.

Early later wrote that he ordered Gordon to advance to gauge the strength of the Union positions. If they

A monument to wounded Confederate general Stephen Ramseur sits along the Valley Pike near the turnoff for Belle Grove. (cm)

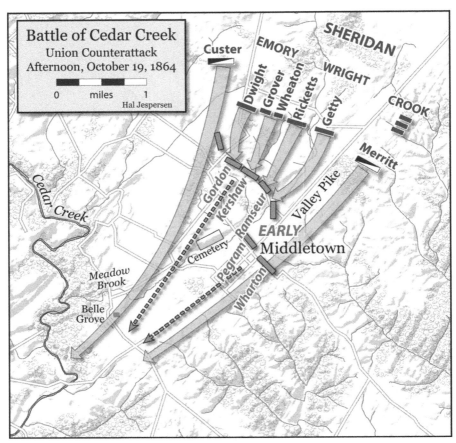

UNION COUNTERATTACKS DURING THE BATTLE OF CEDAR CREEK—The key to Sheridan's counterattack at Cedar Creek was the cavalry division commanded by Brig. Gen. George Custer. Custer's troopers were able to turn the Confederate left flank, which caused a panic among the Rebels that collapsed their line.

proved too strong, the Georgian was to pull back. With the remaining fog of the morning and the smoke of the fight hanging in the air, Early could not distinguish the Union dispositions. In order to reconnoiter and better assess the situation, Early ordered a halt. Old Jube justified the halt because "it was now apparent that it would not do to press my troops further." Their assault had traversed "over rough ground to attack the enemy in the early morning" and the "ranks had been much disordered." When the fog began to lift, it gave Early additional justification by revealing the enemy position along the ridge; it was "discovered to be a strong one," he contended.

Early also explained the halt because of the necessity of dealing "with the threat of Federal cavalry" and

Middletown flooded with the wounded. (wrhs)

"plunderers [of the captured Union camps] returned to the ranks."

However, this was not how John Gordon would remember the fateful lull in the battle. As Gordon arrived for a second conference with the Confederate commander, Early greeted him as cheerfully as his crusty demeanor would allow, nearly coming close to expressing gratitude. "Well, Gordon, this is glory enough for one day," Early boasted, and he remarked that it had been exactly one month since the defeat and retreat after Third Winchester.

"It is very well so far, general," Gordon replied, "but we have one more blow to strike." Gordon wanted to attack the Union VI Corps immediately.

Early refused, and when Gordon's insistence did not change Old Jube's mind, the Georgian remarked, "My heart went into my boots."

Since that fateful halt on October 19 a multitude of accounts surrounding the halt have been published. Each of the participants had a very different recollection and some of the accounts are dipped in bias due to postwar writings and feelings toward the opposite party. Regardless, the Confederate momentum was stopped.

Brig. Gen. Frank Wheaton (loc)

*   *   *

By 7 a.m., the Yankee situation looked bleak. The troops under George Crook and William Emory had been driven from their positions, and Confederates were preparing to continue the assault. Their objective would be to finish off the VI Corps, the only infantry element yet to engage, and crush the Union army.

Col. J. Warren Keifer (loc)

The divisions of Col. J. Warren Keifer and Brig. Gen. Frank Wheaton held off the Confederate onslaught that swept across this field. (dd/pg)

Brig. Gen. George Washington Getty (loc)

As Federal lines collapsed that morning, Horatio Wright sent word back to the VI Corps' temporary commander, Brig. Gen. James Ricketts, to send two divisions up as reinforcements. It was Wright's hope that these men could help buttress Emory's patchwork line. Instead, Ricketts's entire force moved to the aid of the XIX Corps. Arriving as Emory's lines splintered, the VI Corps was forced to redeploy on the ridges west of Meadow Brook and Belle Grove. The Confederate halt that John Gordon wrote of after the war probably aided the VI Corps in allowing them to consolidate their position.

This new position saw Col. J. Warren Keifer deploy his division on the right and Frank Wheaton on the left of Keifer. Colonel Charles Tompkins, head of the corps' artillery, added his batteries to the line. Filing into position, Keifer's and Wheaton's ranks had to open to allow their broken comrades to pass through. Following close behind were the screaming Southern infantry. A low-hanging fog and the dense smoke made visibility difficult for the Yankees, but they opened a blistering fire.

As the divisions of Kershaw and Evans pressed forward—an advance put in motion by Gordon before his conference with Early—the Federals held their ground. A soldier from Wheaton's division remembered,

"Our well-directed fire pushed them back." This stubborn resistance could not hold for long, though, because the Union line was exposed and silhouetted atop the high ground. When Kershaw's brigades began to turn Keifer's flank, the Union veterans began a fighting retreat, reforming to engage their foes at each successive knoll and ridge.

With Keifer and Wheaton being driven from the field, the only Yankee force still intact— the only thing that stood between the Confederates and absolute disaster that morning—was the VI Corps division of George W. Getty. It would be up to Getty's division to stem the enemy advance and buy time for the army to rally. "That peerless band of veterans . . . was to show to the country and to the world, an exhibition of valor . . . above all the grand achievements of the war," a New Yorker in the division later boasted.

Getty positioned his men in along a crest, which also served as Middletown's cemetery. There, his men repulsed three separate Confederate assaults, each with "great slaughter." It was not until the Rebels began to turn the right flank that Getty abandoned the line. Their stand had been enough, though, to extend the life of the Army of the Shenandoah.

Leaving the cemetery behind, the division joined the rest of the army north of Middletown. Also occupying the new line was Alfred Torbert's cavalry. Torbert's troopers had been on the far Union right earlier that morning when Thomas Rosser struck at Cupp's Mill Ford. As the

The VI Corps made a fierce stand among the headstones of Middletown Cemetery, repulsing three Confederate surges. (dd/pg)

While repelling Tarheel attacks in the cemetery, Brig. Gen. Daniel Bidwell was mortally wounded. He died later that evening. (loc)

Sheridan arrived on the battlefield in the nick of time to rally his men. His presence helped to invigorate his army for the rest of the battle. (wrhs)

"The Battle of Cedar Creek" marker is one in a series of fifty-nine commemorative plaques created by the Battlefield Markers Association throughout the 1920s. Historian Douglas Southall Freeman wrote most of the text for the markers. They were the first highway markers in Virginia. (cm)

roar of musketry echoed from the east, Torbert decided to leave one of George Custer's brigades behind to hold Rosser. The rest of the force moved to the sound of the guns. Wesley Merritt's division, along with Col. Alpheus Moore's brigade, held the left of the line near the Valley Turnpike. Custer's remaining brigade supported Merritt. The Union infantry line extended Merritt's right into the fields west of the highway.

At 10:30 that morning, another individual arrived at the new line: Phil Sheridan. Accompanied by several aides, Sheridan had returned from his conference in Washington. Arriving on the field, his presence ignited the smoldering embers of his army into a roaring fire. His men cheered as he rode down the line.

Little Phil had no plans to continue the retreat. "We'll whip them yet," he told his soldiers. "We shall sleep in our old quarters tonight."

*   *   *

Despite their exhausted state, the Confederates launched one more offensive. Manning the positions they had reached after the morning fighting, Early ordered Evans, Kershaw, and Ramseur forward. The time was near 1 p.m. As the infantry advanced and Carter's guns lent their support, the assault aimed for the right-center of the Union line.

When the Confederates entered into range, the Federal line erupted. The fire ripped through the Confederate lines, and the advance stalled. One Union

staff officer later wrote of "volleys [that] seemed fairly to leap from both sides made the woods echo."

With a disparity in numbers, and exposed out in the open, the Confederates could not maintain their position. They withdrew halfway back to the line they had held prior to the assault. Ramseur's men stopped approximately 1,000 feet to the west of the Valley Pike. Kershaw deployed on his left and Evans on Kershaw's left. The firing subsided with the Confederate retreat. Another lull ensued. Some wishful Southern soldiers believed the day's fighting had reached its end. One South Carolinian recalled that the men in the ranks did not have "a dream of the enemy ever being able to rally."

Around 4:00 p.m., the Union infantry began their advance. The critical moment was at hand, and the outcome of the slugfest would determine the battle.

For a time, Stonewall's old soldiers held. Then there, lurking like a panther to the west, was the Union cavalry.

After shifting his troopers back to the right of the line, Custer had been able to push Rosser back to Cupp's Mill Ford. This action put Custer astride the Confederate left flank and in a prime position to attack their rear. About a half hour after the infantry assault commenced, Custer ordered a charge. His mounted soldiers crashed into the Rebels.

With Yankee cavalry upon them, terror quickly spread among the Confederates. Early's army collapsed. Little Phil was true to his word—his men would sleep in their old camps that night.

For Confederates, the race was on to get across Cedar Creek before they were cut off. As at Fisher's Hill and Tom's Brook, their retreat became a panicked rout. The

Hailing from Massachusetts and a graduate of Harvard, Col. Charles Russell Lowell organized the 2nd Massachusetts Cavalry in the autumn of 1862. During the Valley campaign of 1864, he commanded the Reserve Brigade in Wesley Merritt's cavalry division. Wounded early in the fighting, Lowell elected to stay on the field. He was struck again during the Union counterattack and died the next morning. The previous summer, Lowell's brother-in-law had also become a Union casualty. Colonel Robert Gould Shaw died leading the 54th Massachusetts during an assault on Battery Wagner outside Charleston. (wrhs)

Confederate units became horribly mixed, the men trying to find their way to the stream and put as much distance as possible between themselves and the oncoming Yankees. Union cavalry cut into the retiring Southerners.

The saving grace for thousands of Rebels was darkness. A member of Kershaw's staff remembered that soldiers "singly, by twos, and by the half dozens" drifted in through the night, "but such a confusion . . . the officers were as much dazed and lost in confusion as the privates in the ranks." One soldier from the Laurel Brigade regretted that "[i]t was the saddest sight I ever witnessed in the army to see the utter disorganization of Early's command."

During that hasty Confederate retreat, one wagon was trying to remove its charge from the battlefield. Inside lay the mortally wounded Stephen Ramseur. Late in the afternoon, as the North Carolinian was mounting his third horse of the day, a musket ball entered his right side and passed through both lungs. His staff lowered him down, then summoned an ambulance. He was captured as the ambulance tried to cross a stream and the bridge splintered. Ramseur was brought back to Union lines and put in one of the rooms at a plantation called Belle Grove. Surgeons tried to save him, but Ramseur realized the wound was mortal. As his life ebbed away, former classmates and friends came to his deathbed. George Custer, Henry DuPont, and Wesley Merritt all kept vigil throughout the night.

He died the next day at 10:27 a.m., still wishing he could see his newborn child.

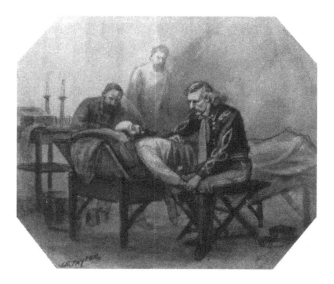

George Custer sat at the bedside of his mortally wounded friend, Stephen Ramseur. (wrhs)

Adjacent to the Cedar Creek battlefield, on land that had been occupied by the VI Corps during the opening stages of the battle, is a quarry operated by a Carmeuse Lime and Stone (pictured in distance). The Belgium company purchased the property, just west of the Belle Grove mansion, in 2008. Prior to Carmeuse's purchase, the quarry had posed an ongoing source of concern for preservations. "Belle Grove and the battlefield have suffered for years from the visual impact of the Chemstone quarry directly behind the 1797 mansion, where a soaring pile of waste and industrial machinery dominate the view," *Civil War News* reported in September 2006, when the quarry petitioned for a zoning change to expand operations. A spokesperson for the American Battlefield Trust lamented, "A mining operation on a battlefield is the worst possible thing." Since Carmeuse acquired the property, however, the company has worked with James Madison University on an archeological survey that has unearthed more than 6,000 artifacts, some of which are on display at the Hupp's Hill Civil War Museum. The company has also donated more than thirty acres to the Cedar Creek Battlefield Foundation. Such partnerships are critical to preserving battlefield lands in the Valley and underscore future preservation successes. (cm)

The End of the Campaign

CHAPTER TWELVE

AUTUMN 1864

The leaves in the Shenandoah Valley had begun to turn color even before the two armies collided at Cedar Creek. After the battle, they were not the only change afoot in the land. The 1864 Valley campaign solidified Union control of a region where Southern armies had run roughshod over Federals during the early stages in the war. Like so much of the South that autumn, it was another place wrenched from the hands of the Confederacy. Much of the credit for this success is owed to Philip Sheridan.

When the value of battlefield victories was immeasurable, Phil Sheridan was thrust into a position where defeat was unacceptable. Intensely aware of that fact, Sheridan committed his forces to combat when the situation was favorable. In September, only when Richard Anderson's reinforcements left Early's army did Sheridan attack. At Fisher's Hill, he meticulously positioned and maneuvered his troops to keep his intentions hidden prior to the attack. The following month, Sheridan dispatched his better-armed and better-led cavalry to stop the harassment of his rear at Tom's Brook.

No small credit can be given to Little Phil's subordinates for these victories. Again, as he had throughout the spring, Sheridan relied heavily upon the skills of the officers serving under him.

Sheridan's plan to advance directly through the Berryville Canyon at Third Winchester caused a bottleneck that put the army in serious harm. Had the Confederates been consolidated, Early could have moved to block the Federal advance. Sheridan's lack of reconnaissance of the Berryville Turnpike nearly doomed

According to the Department of Veterans Affairs, "Winchester National Cemetery was established on land appropriated for burials during the Civil War. Although the land was used for burial purposes as early as 1862, the cemetery was not officially dedicated until April 8, 1866."

(dd/pg)

the VI Corps' assault. If not for the quick actions of David Russell, the attack may have been splintered. Little Phil's over-eagerness after the morning's delay cost Russell his life. George Crook's assault managed to stabilize the situation, allowing for the final Union push later that day.

Sheridan again leaned on Crook's leadership at Fisher's Hill. The results of his assault could not have been better. Praise for these victories must be shared with Crook. At Tom's Brook, George Custer and Wesley Merritt carried the day for the Federals.

However, all these major accomplishments were nearly undone at Cedar Creek.

**Phil Sheridan,
victor of the Valley** (loc)

Since late September, Sheridan had convinced himself the campaign was over. This idea managed to permeate itself through the entire chain of command, all the way down to the lowliest private. The complacency exhibited by the Union army almost resulted in disaster. A Confederate victory at Cedar Creek may have altered the entire campaign. This battle witnessed Sheridan's greatest asset, his ability to inspire men to follow. Borne out on the fields north of Middletown, Sheridan's charismatic and commanding presence uplifted his defeated soldiers. It was a turning point in what was possibly the campaign's most important battle.

Even then, credit must be given to the actions of George Getty. His stand in the Middletown Cemetery allowed a crumbling army to rally. In turn, it allowed the army to launch a devastating counterattack later in the afternoon.

As it turned out at the time, Cedar Creek solidified the reelection of Abraham Lincoln. It guaranteed the war would end on Lincoln's terms. With Atlanta in Union hands, the situation was still stalemated in the war's most important theatre. The capture and destruction of the Shenandoah Valley showed a weary populace that Union fortunes were indeed turning. Its loss proved Jackson's prophetic statement—once the Valley was lost, so too was Virginia. Less than seven full months later, Robert E. Lee surrendered at Appomattox Court House.

The campaign made Philip Sheridan. It catapulted him to a place among William T. Sherman and Ulysses S. Grant as the greatest Union commanders. After the war, Sheridan headed the Department of the Missouri. Ascending to the rank of lieutenant general in 1869, Sheridan became commanding general of the army

Future presidents Rutherford B. Hayes and William McKinley, who started the war together serving in the 23rd Ohio, both parlayed their service into successful bids for the White House. (loc)

in 1884. He would be promoted to full general shortly before his death on August 5, 1888.

While the events in the Valley propelled Sheridan militarily, for others, it benefitted them politically. Rutherford Hayes, who had inspired his men at Third Winchester and performed exceptionally at Fisher's Hill, was elected to Congress during the campaign. He resigned in June 1867 to run for the governorship of Ohio. Resigning after two terms, Hayes lost in a bid to rejoin Congress in 1871. After regaining the governor's seat in 1875, Hayes made a bid for the White House the following year and became the 19th president of the United States.

William McKinley, who carried Crook's attack orders at Third Winchester, ran for Congress the same year Hayes was elected president. He served every term, except one, until his defeat in 1891. Returning home to Ohio, McKinley was elected governor. He served two terms before being elected to the presidency in 1896. He was the last Civil War veteran to hold the office.

*   *   *

As victory rocketed Sheridan to the top echelon of Union leadership of the war, the defeat in the Valley cost Early just as much. After the loss at Cedar Creek, Early's report to Lee included his admission that, if "the interests of the service would be promoted by a change of commanders," Early would accept the decision. He tried in that same report to explain away the reasons behind the campaign's results, but Lee decided Early was right. When the Second Corps left the Valley that autumn and returned to the lines around Richmond and Petersburg, Gordon was its new commander. He would continue on in that role through winter and spring, eventually leading the Army of Northern Virginia on its final march when

The Army of the Shenandoah voted in the presidential election knowing that their success in the autumn campaign had done much to bolster President Lincoln's chances for reelection. (wrhs)

Lee's men laid down their arms at Appomattox Court House on April 9, 1865.

Early, meanwhile, retained command of a token force in the passes of the Blue Ridge until March 2, 1865. During the battle of Waynesboro, George Custer annihilated what was left of the Army of the Valley. Most of the Confederate force surrendered, yet Early and a few other officers escaped. It was the last command Early held during the war.

When Early and Gordon planned assaults, Dr. Hunter Holmes McGuire made preparations to handle the influx of wounded. He was one of the most proficient surgeons the Confederacy had. In May 1863, McGuire had done everything humanly possible to keep Stonewall Jackson alive. After the bloody autumn of 1864, he stayed with the Second Corps for the rest of the war. Afterwards, he served as president of the American Medical Association and as chair of surgery at the Medical College of Virginia. On a trip through Richmond, Virginia, visitors will see the name "McGuire" on buildings and campuses dedicated to the medical world.

In an analysis of the campaign, it would appear logical to place the blame for the Confederate disaster on Early's shoulders. That assumption would be unfair. From the beginning, his army was outnumbered close to two-and-a-half to one. Early had the cream of the Confederate infantry under his command. The Second Corps comprised some of the best units in the Confederacy. Joseph Kershaw's division was also exceptional. Granted, Early's cavalry was not on equal footing with the infantry; at this stage in the war, it was a shell of its former self.

With a disparity in numbers and an inferior mounted arm, Early still turned in a reasonable—if sometimes uneven—performance. His maneuvering in August befuddled Sheridan. Like his antagonist, he put his army in great jeopardy by sending a massed reconnaissance to Stephenson's Depot. If Little Phil had chosen a different access of advance, he might have chewed the Confederates up piecemeal. Old Jube handled his men with poise at Third Winchester, shifting them from one critical area to the next. At the end of the day, numbers prevailed, and his army was driven from the field. Early's actions at Fisher's Hill are inexplicable. He put his weakest troops in a position that required the most strength. It resulted in a complete disaster.

An important aspect that aided Early's soldiers was the fact that they were fighting for their very homes. Numerous regiments hailed from the Shenandoah Valley. This gave additional motivation to defeating the Northern invaders. After suffering severe setbacks at Third Winchester and Fisher's Hill, the Confederates were re-galvanized by "The Burning" and delivered a crushing offensive at Cedar Creek. Indeed, what Early accomplished that morning was more spectacular than any of Stonewall Jackson's great accomplishments. However determined the assault was, though, the lack of numbers and the superiority of Union cavalry won out. There was only so much a determined albeit tired and hungry army could do against a well-rested, well-fed, and better-armed enemy.

*   *   *

For three consecutive years, major campaigns had crisscrossed the lower Shenandoah Valley. The one of 1864 surpassed them all in destruction and devastation. With late autumn approaching and the bleakness of winter to follow, the residents of the area could only wonder what the future would hold.

When Grant had ordered the Valley destroyed, Sheridan's legions effectively laid waste to large tracts of the Valley. Like the Georgia countryside, large swaths of the "Confederate Breadbasket" lay in ruins. One soldier wrote home that within his eyesight "one hundred hay stacks and barns" along with "nearly every farm" were torched.

One Virginia soldier summed up the prevailing attitude of many Valley residents when he wrote, "War is all that can be heard and everybody is tired of it." Another compared life to "like walking through the Valley of the Shadow of Death . . . . [O]ur cause seems to be desperate."

The Confederate cause was desperate indeed. More than 25,000 soldiers had been added to the growing casualty list of the war, attesting to the bloody autumn the Shenandoah Valley witnessed.

At the Winchester National Cemetery, the 8th Vermont monument (below, left) honors men from the regiment who perished during the war. The state of Massachusetts erected a monument (below, right) to honor Bay Staters who fell. Three Massachusetts regiments also erected monuments of their own. Of the fifteen monuments in the cemetery, ten were erected to commemorate soldiers from various New England states. (dd/pg)

Belle Grove (opposite) remains an iconic fixture overlooking the Cedar Creek battlefield. (cm)

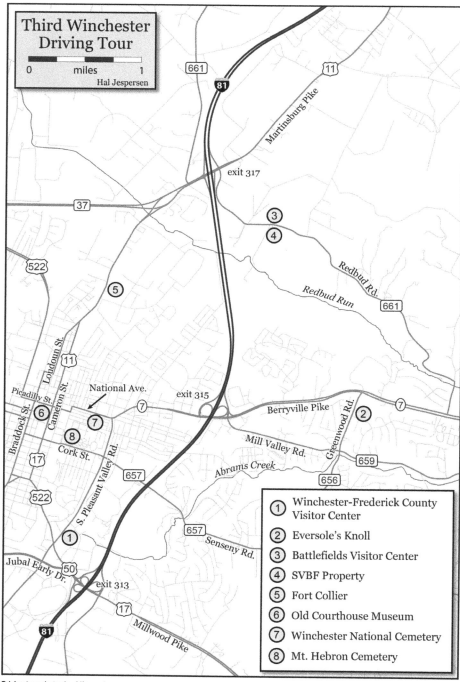

Third Winchester
Driving Tour

0   miles   1

Hal Jespersen

① Winchester-Frederick County
   Visitor Center
② Eversole's Knoll
③ Battlefields Visitor Center
④ SVBF Property
⑤ Fort Collier
⑥ Old Courthouse Museum
⑦ Winchester National Cemetery
⑧ Mt. Hebron Cemetery

Driving tour photos by dd/pg and cm

DRIVING TOUR #1

TOUR STOP 1: Winchester-Frederick County Visitor Center

1400 South Pleasant Valley Road, Winchester, VA, 22601
GPS coordinates: 39.16855° N, 78.16132° W

The Visitor Center is a great place to begin a tour of Third Winchester. Situated near the parking lot is Abrams' Delight, one of oldest homes in Winchester. Construction on the main house began in 1748 by one of the earliest settlers of Frederick County, Abram Hollingsworth. There is a Civil War kiosk inside the visitor center that will orient you to the surrounding area and the actions that took place during both the 1862 and 1864 Valley campaigns. While here, you may gather maps and materials on the Civil War and the surrounding area.

⟶ TO TOUR STOP 2

Leaving the Orientation Center, turn right onto South Pleasant Valley Road. Proceed 1.2 miles to the intersection of Route 7. You will notice Mt. Hebron Cemetery on your left before you reach the intersection. You will come back to this as the last stop on the Third Winchester tour. In the meantime, turn right onto Route 7, the Berryville Turnpike. Proceed 2.3 miles and turn right onto Route 656 (Greenwood Road). Continue up the hill and make a left into the parking lot of the Grace Brethren Church. This is Tour Stop 2. GPS: 39.18582° N, 78.11062° W

TOUR STOP 2: Eversole's Knoll

143 Greenwood Road, Winchester, VA 22602

At the time of battle, this knoll was occupied by the farm of J. A. Eversole. The farm marked the westernmost reaches of the Berryville Canyon. On the morning of the battle, the 2nd and 5th New York Cavalry, supported by the 18th Pennsylvania Cavalry, pushed Robert Johnston's North Carolinians through this area. Johnston was wounded during the engagement.

It was here that Sheridan set up his headquarters on the morning of the battle. Looking east, Little Phil viewed his army marching toward its first large encounter with Early's forces. Was he anxious, realizing that defeat would be costly not only to his army but to the Northern war effort? He could not have known at the time that he would witness on that day the beginning of the end of the Confederate presence in the Shenandoah Valley. From this command post, Sheridan directed the battle. Beyond the Berryville Turnpike and just past the high school, one can still glimpse the fringes of the First Woods.

➤ TO TOUR STOPS 3 & 4

Turn right of out the parking lot and make a right at the stoplight. As you drive through the Berryville Canyon, notice its depth and its sides. After entering the canyon, make the first left, which will take you up a long ramp. Make a left onto Woods Mills Road. Proceed on Woods Mill Road and make another left onto Redbud Road. In approximately 2.4 miles, the parking lot for the James R. Wilkins Winchester Battlefields Visitor Center will be on your left; the visitor center is to the right of the road. GPS: 39.405497°N, -77.444188° W

TOUR STOPS 3 & 4: The James R. Wilkins Winchester Battlefields Visitor Center and Trails
541 Redbud Road, Winchester VA 22603

By driving here, you have traveled through the rear of the Union lines. Stop 3, the Wilkins Winchester Battlefields Visitor Center, provides orientation to the battles fought around Winchester. Across the street, Stop 4 overlooks Early's left flank and offers access to more than 450 preserved acres of the Third Winchester Battlefield. An interlocking series of trails connects you to sites and monuments of the Third Winchester Battlefield. Walk in the footsteps of officers such as Rutherford B. Hayes and Robert Rodes as they fought in the largest battle in the Shenandoah Valley.

TO TOUR STOP 4

Turn left out of the parking lot and proceed on Redbud Road approximately one mile. Turn left at the light onto Route 11 South. Proceed 1.7 miles and make a left onto Brooke Road. As soon as you cross the railroad track, make an immediate left onto a gravel road. This will lead you to the parking area for Fort Collier. GPS: 39.20116° N, 78.15378° W

TOUR STOP 4: Fort Collier
922 Martinsburg Pike,
Winchester, VA 22601

Traveling south on Route 11, you have followed the path that the Union cavalry took during their charge on the fort. At the time of the battle, the ground north of the fort was open and rolling. Brigadier General Wesley Merritt commented that the ground was ideally suited for cavalry operations. It was here that the Confederate line began to give way and collapse.

TO TOUR STOP 5

From Ft. Collier, turn left onto Route 11 and proceed into Winchester. Follow the signs for parking but be mindful that some streets are one-way. The museum is located at 20 North Loudoun Street. GPS: 39.18443° N, 78.16502° W

TOUR STOP 5:
Old Courthouse Museum
20 N Loudoun Street,
Winchester, VA 22601

Downtown Winchester changed hands more than 70 times during the war. The courthouse, constructed in 1840 on the site where the previous courthouse once stood was used either as a courthouse or offices until 1995. The following year, the idea of turning it into a Civil War museum was recommended and seven years later the museum opened its door.
The building saw all visages of the war—first, as a rallying point for local men to sign up to fight for war, then as a place to care for the wounded, and lastly a place to house captured soldiers. Take a tour of the courthouse to learn about Winchester in the Civil War and the museum's collection of artifacts; including some impressive pieces of artillery. Of particular note is the inscriptions that have been verified of soldiers that spent time in the Old Courthouse as prisoners of war, both Northern and Southern.

TO TOUR STOP 6

After returning to your car, proceed to Route 7 (East). Follow the signs to the Winchester National Cemetery. Be careful pulling into the cemetery. Parking is limited. GPS: 39.18432° N, 78.15653° W

TOUR STOP 6: Winchester National Cemetery
401 National Avenue, Winchester, VA 22601

Remember, this is a place of reverence. Please follow the cemetery regulations posted at the gate.

There are many monuments to explore in the cemetery. Notice the monument to the 114th New York Infantry. This regiment lost more than 60 percent of their strength while stopping Maj. Gen. John Gordon's counterattack from the Second Woods at Winchester. Farther down on the right as you walk from the parking lot is a monument to the 34th Massachusetts Infantry. The bust on top of the monument is the regiment's commander, Col. George Wells (see page 61). He was killed during a skirmish a few days before the battle of Cedar Creek. From the National Cemetery, you can see Mt. Hebron Cemetery across the street, where a number of Confederates were buried.

➤ TO TOUR STOP 7:

Make a left out of the cemetery onto Route 7. Make another left onto North East Lane. The entrance to Mt. Hebron Cemetery will be on the left. Once you enter the cemetery gates, follow the signs to the Confederate section of the cemetery. Again, this is a place of reverence. GPS: 39.18197° N, 78.15792° W

TOUR STOP 7: Mt. Hebron Cemetery
305 East Boscawen Street, Winchester, VA 22601

The cemetery is actually four cemeteries surrounded by one enclosure and in the oldest section graves date from 1769. In 1844 the charter was granted by the General Assembly of Virginia in response to a petition by the people of Frederick County "to establish a public cemetery." As you drive in, follow signs to the "Stonewall" Cemetery where Confederate dead are buried. Next to the cemetery road, you will find the graves of Robert Johnston, Archibald Godwin, and George Patton. All three men fought at Third Winchester. Johnston was

The grave of Confederate cavalryman Turner Ashby, who was killed in a skirmish outside Harrisonburg in June of 1862 during Stonewall Jackson's '62 Valley campaign

wounded and Godwin was killed. Patton was mortally wounded during the fight. Following the battle, he was taken to a house in Winchester owned by his cousin, Mary Williams, where he passed away on September 25. Patton was interred in the same grave as his brother, Tazewell, after the war. As a colonel of the 7th Virginia Infantry, Tazewell was killed in Pickett's Charge at Gettysburg.

This concludes the driving tour for Third Winchester.

Col. George S. Patton and his brother, Tazewell, were both mortally wounded during the war—the former at Third Winchester and latter at Gettysburg. They share a gravesite. "Here lie asleep in one grave The Patton Brothers," their headstone says.

Prior to his wounding at Third Winchester, Confederate Brig. Gen. Robert Johnston had been wounded three times during the war: Seven Pines, Gettysburg, and Spotsylvania. He surived the war, however, and practiced law in North Carolina until his death in 1919.

Maj. Gen. Daniel Morgan, a hero of the Revolutionary War and a key figure in supressing the Whiskey Rebellion, retired to Winchester, where he represented the area in Congress as a Federalist. He died at his daughter's home on his sixty-sixth birthday.

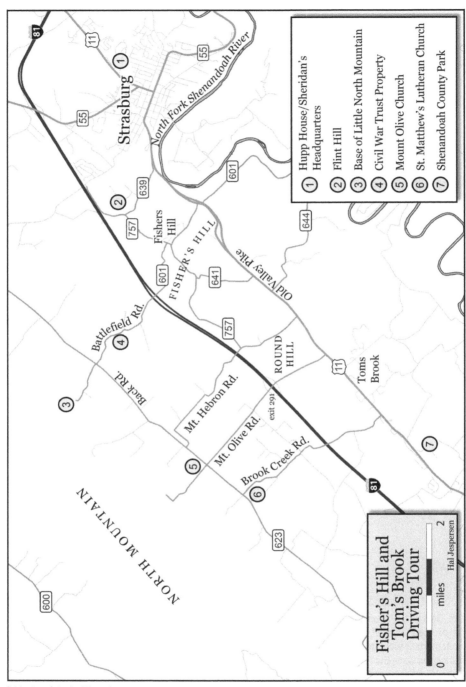

Fisher's Hill and
Tom's Brook
Driving Tour

1 Hupp House/Sheridan's Headquarters
2 Flint Hill
3 Base of Little North Mountain
4 Civil War Trust Property
5 Mount Olive Church
6 St. Matthew's Lutheran Church
7 Shenandoah County Park

Hal Jespersen

Driving tour photos by dd/pg and cm

DRIVING TOUR #2

Please be aware that many of the roads on the driving tour are narrow and winding. Use extreme caution.

Cedar Creek and Belle Grove
National Historical Park Visitor Contact Station

7710 Main Street, Middletown, VA 22645
GPS coordinates: 39.03118° N, 78.27557° W

The National Park Service Visitor Contact Station at Cedar Creek and Belle Grove National Historic Site is the starting point for tours of Fisher's Hill, Tom's Brook, and Cedar Creek. Inside there are exhibits on the battle of Cedar Creek along with other aspects of the war in the Shenandoah Valley. If you are going to tour the Cedar Creek battlefield, please refer to page 103.

▷ TO TOUR STOP 1

Leaving the Visitor Contact Station, turn left onto Route 11. Follow Route 11 south for 5 miles. You will cross Cedar Creek and pass Burger King and Arby's. After passing the drug store on the left, you will see a circular driveway to a brick house with large white columns. This is Tour Stop 1. Please stay in your vehicle after you pull into the driveway. GPS: 38.99594° N, 78.35340° W

TOUR STOP 1: Hupp House / Sheridan's Headquarters

This house served as Maj. Gen. Philip Sheridan's headquarters prior to the battle. In the front yard, Sheridan called a council of war to discuss plans for attacking Fisher's Hill. Prior to the conference, Maj. Gen. George Crook reconnoitered the left of the

Confederate position. Finding the flank vulnerable and a means to move a large force under cover to assail it, he made his proposal. Crook called upon his two division commanders, Cols. Rutherford Hayes and Joseph Thoburn, to lend their weight to the argument. Their views prevailed.

▶ **TO TOUR STOP 2**

Turn left onto Route 11. Proceed to the first stoplight in Strasburg. Turn right at the light. Proceed 1.9 miles and make a right onto Battlefield Road. Proceed 0.8 miles and make a right onto Green Acres Drive (the "Battlefield Drive" signage here can be confusing). Drive past the brown sign marked "Battlefield" on the right and, after 0.1 miles, make a sharp right-hand turn onto Church Hill Lane. Drive to the top of the hill to the parking lot. This is Tour Stop 2. GPS: 38.98580° N, 78.37930° W

TOUR STOP 2: Flint Hill

Off to the right front is a bald hill called "Ramseur's Hill," named for Confederate Maj. Gen. Stephen Ramseur, whose troops held the position. The eminence you are standing on is known as Flint Hill. Here, Sheridan observed the attack on the Confederate bastion. On September 21, this ground was held by Rebel skirmishers. During the

deployment prior to the engagement, Sheridan ordered Maj. Gen. Horatio Wright to seize this position. Wright chose the 126th Ohio and 139th Pennsylvania Infantry to make the assault. Confederate resistance here was stiff and the Pennsylvanians lost their commander, Maj. Robert Munroe. After the repulse, the 6th Maryland was brought forward to reinforce their comrades. This attack was also turned back. On a third try, Col. James Warner's Union brigade finally captured the position.

▶ **TO TOUR STOP 3**

Turn left from the parking lot. At the first stop sign, make a right and follow the brown "Battlefield" signs. The high ground to your right was held by Wright's VI Corps. Wright's men would attack the Confederates atop Fisher's Hill to your left as you are driving through the valley. Continue past the American

Battlefield Trust property to the intersection of Battlefield Road and the Back Road. Approximately 1.5 miles to your right, the march of the Army of West Virginia reached Little North Mountain at St. Stephen's Church. Although it is not on the driving tour, feel free to travel to this location. At the stop sign, proceed straight onto the gravel road and continue 0.6 miles to its end. Turn your vehicle around in the circle. GPS: 39.00001° N, 78.43094° W

TOUR STOP 3:
Little North Mountain

You are now on the crest of Little North Mountain. Looking through the trees to your left, you can see the approach route that the "Mountain Creepers" took along its base. The house and property are private, so please respect the owners' rights. Crook's divisions reached this vicinity around 3 p.m. on the afternoon of September 22. In the

woods to your right, Hayes and Thoburn formed for the assault. As you proceed to Tour Stop 4, you will be roughly following the attack of the Army of West Virginia.

➤ TO TOUR STOP 4

Return to the Back Road. As you reach the intersection, notice the ridge to your immediate right front. This was the Confederate left flank and the target of Crook's assault. Retrace your route to the American Battlefield Trust property. GPS: 38.98583° N, 78.39969° W

TOUR STOP 4: American Battlefield Trust Property

This is known as Ramseur's Hill, the location you viewed from Tour Stop 2. Follow the mowed path. There are six stops along the path that provide excellent interpretation into the flow of the battle, while providing maps to show where you are on the battlefield, as you climb the hill. Brochures are provided for reference.

As you reach the top of the hill, you are walking along part of the line held by Brig. Gen. Bryan Grimes' brigade. Ramseur ordered Grimes to pull men out of the main line to help stem the Union advance. Grimes positioned the 32nd and 45th North Carolina Infantry and the 2nd North Carolina Battalion to face the attack coming from Little North Mountain. Another brigade of North Carolinians, commanded by Brig. Gen. William Cox, moved to support Grimes but got lost amongst the terrain. Cox' Tarheels did not participate in the battle.

Grimes' resistance was futile and they were overrun by the Mountain Creepers and the attacking VI Corps division of Brig. Gen. James Ricketts.

This is ends the tour for Fisher's Hill.

 TO TOUR STOP 5

To begin the tour of Tom's Brook, return to the Back Road. Turn left and proceed 2.2 miles to Mount Olive Church. The church is on the left side at the intersection of the Back Road and Mount Olive Road (State Route 651). GPS: 38.97854° N, 78.45707° W

TOUR STOP 5: Mount Olive Church

Driving to this stop, you have followed the footsteps of Brig. Gen. George Custer's division as they moved to engaged Brig. Gen. Thomas Rosser's division on the morning of the battle. Colonel Alexander Pennington's brigade led the march, followed by Col. William Wells' brigade. Here at the intersection, the 5th New York Cavalry opened the battle by engaging pickets from the 4th Virginia Cavalry. The New Yorkers slowly pushed the Virginians back to their main line on Spiker's Hill.

A non-Civil War marker sits alongside the road between Mount Olive Church and St. Matthew's: Frieden's Monument, erected in 1945 by the Hottel-Keller Memorial Association to mark the location of a school and church. Frieden's, "a Union Church, Evangelical Lutheran and German Reformed," was dedicated in 1824 and vacated in 1877.

 TO TOUR STOP 6

Continue on the Back Road for 0.8 miles. Turn left onto Sand Ridge Road and drive to St. Matthew's Lutheran Church. Pull into the parking lot, get out of your vehicle, and walk to the far right corner of the parking lot near the fence. GPS: 38.96725° N, 78.46591° W

TOUR STOP 6: St. Matthew's Lutheran Church

Directly ahead of you is Spiker's Hill, the position held by Rosser's cavalry. In the treeline at the bottom of the hill is Tom's Brook. From your vantage point, the 4th Virginia Cavalry was positioned at the base of the hill where the Back Road crossed the stream. Above them on the hill, from your right to left, was the 1st, 2nd, and 3rd Virginia Cavalry. Continuing along the hill to your left, Rosser positioned the brigade of Col. William Payne. The "Laurel Brigade" was positioned on Payne's right.

Custer initiated the fighting by sending Pennington in a mounted charge through the area you are standing in. Pennington sent the 5th New York, 3rd New Jersey, and 2nd Ohio forward to the stream. There, they were met by the 12th Virginia and 35th Virginia Cavalry Battalion and driven back. Custer then committed the 18th Pennsylvania in an attack along the Back Road. The Pennsylvanians were met by the 4th Virginia, reinforced by the 1st, 2nd, and 3rd Virginia and repulsed.

Receiving word that Col. James Kidd's Michigan Brigade was on the way to reinforce his left, Custer decided to bring up Wells' regiments. The 8th and 22nd New York, from William Wells' brigade, along with the 18th Pennsylvania, would move around to strike Rosser's left flank. As a diversion, the 1st New Hampshire and 1st Vermont engaged the Confederate front. During the ensuing attack,

Custer personally led the 5th New York in a charge up Spiker's Hill. With the New Yorkers and Keystoners pressing his left and Kidd's Michiganders his right, Rosser's line collapsed and Custer won the day.

TO TOUR STOP 7

Turn right out of the church parking lot onto Sand Ridge Road. Follow Sand Ridge Road to the intersection of Brook Creek Road. Make a right on Brook Creek Road and follow it for 1.3 miles until you reach the Valley Turnpike. Make a right on Valley Turnpike. After 0.7 miles, you will see a Civil War Trails sign ahead. Make a left-hand turn into Shenandoah County Park. Follow the Civil War Trails sign and drive out around the far side of the tennis courts. Park your car and walk out to the sign, which is on the crest of the far ridge past the small picnic pavilion. GPS: 38.93526° N, 78.45377° W

TOUR STOP 7: Shenandoah County Park

You are standing at Maj. Gen. Lunsford Lomax' position, and the hill ahead with the cell tower is Round Hill. From this position, Sheridan observed the battle. Lomax positioned the brigade of William Thompson to your left, across Route 11. Brigadier

General Bradley Johnson extended the line to the east. The 2nd Maryland Battery was positioned on the turnpike. These brigades engaged Brig. Gen. Wesley Merritt's Reserve Brigade, commanded by Col. Charles Russell Lowell. After repulsing Lomax' thrust, Lowell led his old regiment, the 2nd Massachusetts Cavalry, against the Confederate line. Off to your left, the 1st New York Dragoons and the 5th U.S. Cavalry began to turn Lomax' flank. This maneuver forced the Confederates to abandon their line and withdraw. Pursued by the Federals, the withdrawal quickly became a rout.

This concludes the driving tour for Tom's Brook.

1 NPS Visitor Contact Station
2 Cedar Creek Battlefield Foundation HQ
3 Eighth Corps Camps
4 Bowman's Mill Ford
5 Long Meadow
6 128th New York Monument
7 8th Vermont Monument
8 Belle Grove
9 Mt. Carmel Cemetery
10 Miller's Mill
11 Sheridan's Arrival
12 Union Counterattack

Middletown

Strasburg

exit 302

Cedar Creek Driving Tour

0   miles   1

Hal Jespersen

Driving tour photos by dd/pg and cm

Cedar Creek
DRIVING TOUR #3

This driving tour follows portions of but does not replicate completely the National Park Service driving tour for the battlefield.

TOUR STOP 1: Cedar Creek and Belle Grove National Historical Park Visitor Contact Station

7710 Main Street, Middletown, VA 22645
GPS coordinates: 39.03118° N, 78.27557° W

At the visitor contact station, pick up maps, brochures, and information about the battle of Cedar Creek. Tours are offered seasonally, so you can inquire about them if you have the opportunity. Exhibits and an illuminated battle map highlight the battle of Cedar Creek coupled with displays about the history of the Shenandoah Valley and the Civil War in the region.

 TO TOUR STOP 2

Turn left out of the contact station parking lot and proceed 1.5 miles south. Cedar Creek Battlefield Association Headquarters will be on your left. GPS: 39.01604° N, 78.29623° W

TOUR STOP 2: Cedar Creek Battlefield Association Headquarters

8437 Valley Pike Middletown, VA 22645

Situated on the vital Valley Pike (present day VA Route 11), the stop here is directly across from the fields around Belle Grove. The Union army's sprawling encampment was spread through this area.

Prior to the formation of Cedar Creek and Belle Grove National Historical Park and the opening of the National Park Service visitor contact station, the Cedar Creek Battlefield Association was the organization that worked to preserve the battlefield. They have continued in operation and still have their headquarters with a small bookstore and information here at this location. *One of the later stops on the driving tour will be at the entrenchments of the Union XIX Corps. To hike these entrenchments, please get permission at this stop.*

 TO TOUR STOP 3

Turn left out of the association's parking lot. Proceed one mile south on the Valley Pike and make the left on Water Plant Road. Proceed one mile to the intersection with Long Meadow Road (note: at the intersection, Water Plant Road will change names to Gafia Lodge Road). Turn right onto Long Meadow Road. In approximately .01 mile, turn right onto Bowman's Mill Road. Proceed 1.4 miles down Bowman's Mill Road. The road has several sharp elbow turns; the stop will be after a sharp bend in the road to the left. Signage will state "No Trespassing" and "Shenandoah Valley Battlefield Foundation." There is a Civil War Trails sign at the stop. Pull over to the right of the road where a little pull-off is located. Permission can be attained ahead of time to access this property; otherwise please do not wander into the fields. GPS: 38.99884° N, 78.31960° W

Tour Stop 3: Camps of the Army of West Virginia

You are now at the extreme left of the Union line, which was manned by Maj. Gen. George Crook's Army of West Virginia. Confederates under Maj. Gen. John Gordon's command crossed from beyond Crook's left, turning their position and striking the

exposed left flank. The division of Maj. Gen. Joseph Kershaw came up the road to assault the Federals. With the first attacks happening as dawn arrived and heavy fog blanketed the area, these attacks surprised and then routed the Union defenders. Imagine, as a Union soldier, you are about to rise to breakfast, thinking the enemy is miles away, when thousands of Confederates, screaming the blood-stopping "Rebel Yell" descend on your encampments. What would your reaction be?

 TO TOUR STOP 4

Continue in same direction on Bowman's Mill Road and, in 0.6 miles, stay to the right to continue on Bowman's Mill Road. In front of you as you come down the hill will be Cedar Creek and the general area where the Confederates crossed. GPS: 38.99107° N, 78.32801° W

Tour Stop 4: Bowman's Mill Ford

On the morning of October 19, 1864, approximately 2,500 soldiers of Joseph Kershaw's division crossed here. The Southerners quickly overran the 5th New York Heavy Artillery guarding the ford and deployed for battle in the field around you. When Kershaw's men came on line, they advanced toward Tour Stop 4.

➤ TO TOUR STOP 5

Proceed back up the hill and make the right onto Long Meadow Road. To your right is Cedar Creek and 1.2 miles down the road Cedar Creek will merge with the North Fork of the Shenandoah River. Continue on for another 0.2 miles and immediately following the driveway of Long Meadow farm—which is privately owned and not open to the public—pull your vehicle to the right side of the road.

GPS: 38.98487° N, 78.30330° W

Tour Stop 5: Long Meadow

In this general area stood a log cabin, built by Jost Hite and later occupied by his son Isaac. This family could claim to be some of the first settlers in the lower Shenandoah Valley. The majority of the Confederate attacking force, consisting of Gordon's flanking column, crossed here. Gordon's old division, under Clement Evans, crossed first followed by Stephen Ramseur. John Pegram followed Ramseur. The men continued to march in column as they headed northwest before deploying for the assault. Shortly after 5:00 a.m. Gordon launched these three divisions—two in the front line, Evans and Ramseur, with Pegram in support—at Rutherford Hayes' division. The men who advanced here were some of the best combat troops the Confederacy could muster by the autumn of 1864. If victory could be achieved, these would be the men to accomplish it. Follow their march and attack as you head to the next tour stop.

➤ TO TOUR STOP 6

Continue on Long Meadow Road approximately 0.9 miles. At the intersection, turn left onto Water Plant Road. When that road comes up to the intersection of the Valley Pike, turn right to head north. Before turning, the 128th New York Monument may be visible to you across the road depending on the time of year of your visit. Note, you will be on the Valley Pike for less than a 10th of a mile and will be making a left onto a gravel road. GPS: 39.008832° N, 78.309893°W

Tour Stop 6: 128th New York Monument

Hailing from the Empire State, the 128th New York drew the assignment of holding the left flank of the XIX Corps. Surging Confederates, fresh off of wrecking Crook, approached the New Yorkers and lapped around to the rear. On top of this, a second Confederate force, Kershaw's division, was moving in for an attack on their front. What did the 128th New York do? They hugged their entrenchments, loaded their rifles and made a determined stand. Losing their brigade commander, Col. Daniel McCauley, they hung on for the better part of an hour before being overrun and like other retreating bluecoats headed toward Belle Grove, your next stop.

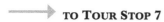 **TO TOUR STOP 7**

Turn left out of the gravel turnout on to Route 11 North. In approximately 0.2 miles, turn right into the driveway just prior to the National Park Service Cedar Creek and Belle Grove Headquarters Parking lot. Proceed up the driveway to the parking area near a white one-story house. The trail to the monument begins to your left front. GPS: 39.405518° N, -77.444179° W

TOUR STOP 7: 8th Vermont Trails
8739 Valley Pike, Middletown, VA 22645

The trail goes down a decline and up to a ridge where the 8th Vermont Monument was placed. On this bluff in the morning of October 19, the 8th Vermont made a sacrificial stand to stem the tide of the Confederate advance, losing 106 of 175 men and 13 of 16 commissioned officers. The monument was a gift from a veteran who survived.

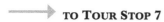 **TO TOUR STOP 8**

Proceed down the driveway and turn right onto Route 11 North. In 0.4 miles, turn left onto Belle Grove Road and follow for approximately a half-mile. The parking lot for the home and grounds will be to your right. GPS: 39.02068° N, 78.30399° W

TOUR STOP 8: Belle Grove
336 Belle Grove Rd, Middletown, VA 22645

As you turn onto Belle Grove Road, to your immediate right will be the monument dedicated to Stephen Dodson Ramseur. Erected in 1919 by the North Carolina Historical Commission and The North Carolina Division United Daughters of the Confederacy, the monument reads, in part, that it stands 800 yards from where

Ramseur died on October 20. One notable person in attendance when the monument was dedicated was Mary Dodson Ramseur, the daughter the late general never met. Be careful if you stop as the monument sits in close proximity to the Valley Pike.

Continue down the road and Belle Grove will come into your view off to your left front. Follow signs to the parking area. To inquire about tours of Belle Grove and other programs being offered, head toward the gift shop.

Belle Grove, built in 1797, stood as the plantation home of Isaac Hite, Jr., a grandson of the Hites from the log cabin history at Long Meadow. Isaac married into the family of President James Madison.

Prior to the battle, Belle Grove served as Philip Sheridan's headquarters. At the beginning of the battle, Sheridan was still returning from a conference in Washington and had only made it as far as Winchester the night before. Union soldiers, pushed back from their first lines of defense, made a stubborn resistance here before Confederates were able to push the bluecoats from the fields and hillocks surrounding the plantation manor.

After the battle, Belle Grove transformed from a scene of killing to a scene of healing as scores of wounded were gathered from around the grounds and manor house. One of the Confederates brought to the main floor was the mortally wounded Stephen Dodson Ramseur. After Ramseur died, his body was taken to his hometown of Lincolnton, North Carolina, for burial. Ramseur was the second division commander of Early's army to die during the campaign; the first was Maj. Gen. Robert Rodes, who was killed at Third Winchester.

▶ **TO TOUR STOP 9**

Turn right out of the parking lot at Belle Grove and proceed less than 0.1 miles. Turn right onto Meadows Mill Road and follow this road for 0.8 miles. Take the left onto Veterans Road and continue on for 0.25 miles. The high ground you are traversing was held by the VI Corps divisions of J. Warren Keifer and Frank Wheaton. Here, they engaged Kershaw's and Evans' attacking Confederations. Make a right onto State Route 635, and the cemetery is located 0.3 miles down this road. GPS: 39.03197° N, 78.28645° W

TOUR STOP 9: Mount Carmel Cemetery

When visiting the cemetery, it is encouraged by the cemetery's management to park in the gravel parking area outside the confines of the cemetery and walk in. Proceed to near the white cinderblock building to get a feel for the grounds. Please be respectful of the cemetery as it is still active, and there could be a funeral procession that would close the area to the public.

Around the headstones, Union soldiers made a determined stand for 90 minutes. Fitting of his name, Brig. Gen. George Washington Getty's division slowed the Confederate avalanche coming towards them. Getty deployed his men as Keifer and Wheaton

attempted to hold back the enemy advance. From right to left, Getty placed the brigades of James Warner, Lewis Grant, and Daniel Bidwell. Here, Getty repulsed assaults by John Pegram's division, elements of the 43rd, 45th, and 53rd North Carolina infantry, and 2nd North Carolina Battalion of Bryan Grimes's brigade and Gabriel Wharton's division. After repulsing these attacks and weathering a 30-minute bombardment from artillery, the Federals pulled back. The defense was crucial to arresting the momentum of the Confederate offensive that morning.

 TO TOUR STOP 10

Proceed .03 miles down High Street. Turn right onto Chapel Road but take a quick left in approximately 0.1 miles onto Mineral Street. Travel down Mineral Street for a half-mile to Miller's Mill. Park the car just past the intersection of Mineral Street and Cougill Road, but since Miller's Mill is privately owned, it is best to stay in your car. GPS: 39.03884° N, 78.27319° W

TOUR STOP 10: Miller's Mill

You are looking at the high-water mark of the Confederate advance at Cedar Creek. Early organized his line here along Miller Lane (present day Cougill Road), and as he did so, soldiers began to leave the line and return to the captured Union encampments. In search of supplies, other impedimenta of war, and more importantly food, their wanderings depleted the strength of the Confederate line. Many of Early's men had not eaten that morning and barely had anything of substance for quite a while—basic needs prevailed. A sense that the day was already won might have convinced others to leave ranks to satisfy growling stomachs. The knoll to your left is also where Stephen Ramseur was mortally wounded during the Federal counterattack later that afternoon.

 TO TOUR STOP 11

Continue down Cougill Road and continue on for 0.8 miles. Turn right onto Hite Road and proceed 0.9 miles. Take the right onto Klines Mill Road and the stop will be 0.9 miles down. The small waterway you pass over, Meadow's Brook, is the site where Sheridan came upon his army, after his ride from Winchester. After crossing the bridge, you can park your car on the right side in the gravel area. As there is not much space here, it may be best to stay in your vehicle.

GPS: 39.05297° N, 78.26291° W

TOUR STOP 11: Sheridan's Arrival

It was here that the most famous aspect of the battle of Cedar Creek occurred. Phil Sheridan returned to the Shenandoah Valley the night before following a council of war in Washington. Seeing no reason to push on the final 15 miles, he spent the night in Winchester. The following morning Sheridan was alerted by sounds of gunfire and artillery to the south. Mounting his horse, Rienzi, he began what is now known as "Sheridan's Ride," reaching the location you are now at around 10:30 a.m. Sheridan's appearance uplifted the men's spirits. Captain William McKinley, the future U.S. president, then serving on George Crook's staff, recommended that Sheridan ride down the length of his line so his men could see him. The response from his men stirred their broken spirits. Preparations were made for a counterattack. The Union army had already weathered the worst of the Confederate offensive by the time Sheridan arrived. However, the importance of his presence on the morale of his soldiers cannot be overlooked.

➤ TO TOUR STOP 12

Continue on Klines Mill Road approximately 0.5 miles, and when you reach the Valley Pike turn right. In 1.4 miles, turn left onto Skirmisher Lane, the third of the entrances to Lord Fairfax Community College. There is a historical marker located at the western end of the parking lot near the Valley Pike titled "Battle of Cedar Creek." Parking close to the southern end of the community college is encouraged as that will put you in the best location in reference to the Union counterattack. One item to note: being a community college, the parking lots fill quickly on school days. GPS: 39.03544° N, 78.26857° W

TOUR STOP 12: Union Counterattack
173 Skirmisher Lane, Middletown, VA 22645

If you look off to your right (if one is facing south), the Miller house is visible in the distance. This area marks where the Confederate line ran through in the early afternoon of October 19. Around 4 p.m., Sheridan ordered a counterattack, and Union soldiers advanced into the fields around you and struck the Confederate line. Though outnumbered, the Confederates put up a stiff resistance. Overwhelming numbers and Union cavalry attacking the line's left flank caused the line to cave in. The Confederates disintegrated from the west to the east. Victory, within the grasp of the Southerners, turned into a disastrous defeat as Early's army raced to safety. The Union secured their grasp on the lower Shenandoah Valley.

Somewhere in this general area, Col. Charles Russell Lowell was mortally wounded (see page 79).

This concludes the driving tour for Cedar Creek.

A 23

BATTLE OF FISHER'S HILL

HERE EARLY'S ADJUTANT-GEN-
ERAL, A. S. PENDLETON, WHILE AT-
TEMPTING TO CHECK SHERIDAN'S
ADVANCE, WAS MORTALLY WOUND-
ED, SEPTEMBER 22, 1864.

CONSERVATION & DEVELOP
MENT COMMISSION 1930

Two Fallen Officers:

Alexander Pendleton
and John Rodgers Meigs

DRIVING TOUR #4

This appendix is meant to bring attention to two additional driving tour stops of interest. Due to their remote locations, they are not included in the main driving tours. The stops address the death of an officer from each army, Alexander "Sandie" Pendleton and John Rodgers Meigs.

John R. Meigs was born on February 9, 1842, in Washington D.C. to Montgomery and Louisa Meigs. His father was an engineer in the U.S. Army and John spent much of his childhood traveling from one post to the next. Young Meigs was appointed to the U.S. Military Academy at West Point in September 1859 and graduated first in the Class of 1863. Being at the top of the class, he received a commission as first lieutenant in the Corps of Engineers. His first assignment was to oversee the construction of defenses for the city of Baltimore. In July 1863, he transferred to the staff of Brig. Gen. Benjamin Franklin Kelley, the commander of the Department of West Virginia. Meigs served briefly with Kelley before transferring to the staff of Brig. Gen. William Averell. On November 6, 1863, Meigs fought at the battle of Droop Mountain and, that December, participated in the Salem Raid. In the spring and summer of 1864, Meigs fought at New Market, Piedmont, and Lynchburg. When Phil Sheridan took command of the Middle Military Division, Meigs

Lt. John R. Meigs (wrhs)

became its chief engineer. For his actions at Third Winchester and Fisher's Hill, Meigs was brevetted to captain and major, respectively.

On October 3, 1864, while leading a surveying party near the town of Dayton, Meigs ran into a group of Confederates. In the ensuring firefight, Meigs was killed. His body was removed and taken to rest in the new military burying ground on Robert E. Lee's estate, Arlington. Earlier that year, Meigs' father, now the quartermaster general for the entire Federal army, recommended using the estate as a cemetery. Today, Arlington National Cemetery is America's most hallowed ground.

Today, a lonely monument stands atop a knoll near the location where Meigs was killed. To reach the Meigs Monument in Dayton, take Route 42 south from

Harrisonburg. Proceed approximately 3.4 miles. Turn left onto Meigs Lane. There is a pull off on the opposite side of the road. Be careful parking your car, as the monument is situated within an industrial park. The monument is just up the knoll from the Civil War Trails sign.

GPS Coordinates: 38° N 25.433', W 78° 55.309'

*   *   *

Alexander Swift "Sandie" Pendleton was born in Alexandria, Virginia, on September 28, 1840, to William Nelson and Anzelotte Elizabeth Pendleton. He spent most of his childhood in Maryland until his father, an Episcopal minister, accepted the ministerial position at Grace Church in Lexington, Virginia. "Sandie" graduated from Washington College in 1857 and was studying for a graduate degree at the University of Virginia when the Civil War broke out. Commissioned a second lieutenant in the Provisional Army of Virginia, the young Pendleton marched off to Harper's Ferry (his father would serve as a brigadier general in the Confederate artillery). An old acquaintance from Lexington, Thomas J. Jackson, soon to become immortalized as "Stonewall," was in charge at Harper's Ferry, and he requested Sandie to be his ordinance officer. Pendleton showed a dedication to the Southern cause that rivaled that of his chief, and his skill as a staff officer impressed Jackson, who directed inquiries to him because "if Pendleton does not know, no one does!"

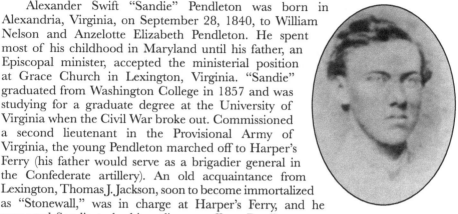

Col. Alexander Swift "Sandie" Pendleton (cm)

Pendleton became Jackson's chief of staff and served with him until Jackson's death on May 10, 1863, following the battle of Chancellorsville. He continued his service on the staff of Jackson's successor, Lt. Gen. Richard Ewell. When Lt. Gen. Jubal Early assumed command of the Second Corps in May 1864, he named Pendleton his chief of staff and promoted him to lieutenant colonel.

After the Confederate defeat at Fisher's Hill, Pendleton was active in trying to organize the chaos of the retreating Southern army. Along with Generals Gordon, Ramseur, and Pegram, Pendleton helped organize a rearguard on a hill near the town of Mount Prospect, approximately 10 miles from Fisher's Hill. There in the darkness, eerily similar to the conditions around Chancellorsville a year earlier that had led to Jackson's wounding, the Federals bumped into the hastily organized Confederate line. The two sides exchanged several volleys until darkness enveloped the area and ended the fighting. Yet, the dying would continue. One of the shots fired by a Union soldier struck Sandie in the abdomen—a type of wound that was almost always fatal. Dr. Hunter McGuire, the chief medical officer of the Second Corps, administered what aid he could. Pendleton lingered until the next day, but that evening he died of his wounds in the nearby town of Woodstock. Pendleton passed away several days shy of his 24th birthday. He left behind a wife of 10 months, Kate, who was pregnant with their first child.

When passing through Lexington the following month, Reverend Dr. D. L. Dabney, who had also served on Jackson's staff, remarked to Pendleton's widow that he felt immune to grief as he had lost so many friends during the war. When told of Sandie's death, Dabney was astonished at the "amount of sorrow I felt." Another staff officer, Henry Kyd Douglas, wrote "his loss is universally felt . . . . I shall miss him every

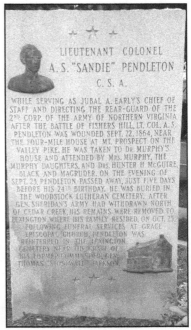

The monuments marking the location of Meigs' mortal wounding (left) and Pendleton's (right) (dd/pg)

A state historical marker along the Valley Pike marking the vicnity of Pendleton's wounding (previous overleaf) (cm)

day, for he was the warmest friend I had in the army." Pendleton was initially buried in Woodstock. A month later, his remains were moved to Lexington and laid to rest near the remains of his former commanding officer.

A monument stands near the location of the house Pendleton was taken to after receiving his mortal wound, although the house itself no longer stands. To reach the site, take I-81 south to exit 283 and then proceed on Route 42 east toward Woodstock and the Valley Pike (Route 11). Turn left onto Route 11 and take the Valley Pike north into Woodstock. Take a left on West Spring Street and then a right onto South Muhlenberg Street. The monument will be on your left near the Woodstock United Methodist Church.

GPS coordinates: N 38° 88.150', W 78° 50.767'

Winchester During the War

APPENDIX A

"[O]n the eve of the Civil War Winchester dominated the lower Shenandoah Valley." So knew residents, military officials, politicians—and now historians.

Even before the war, Winchester had a place in American history. Prior to European settlement, Native Americans passed through the area on the "Warriors Path" to hunt and reach trading partners. After Europeans arrived and settled Winchester, named Frederick Town, the road running through it from north to south became the "Great Wagon Road." More settlers arrived from the area east of the Blue Ridge Mountains or they came down from northern colonies. The only English aristocrat to make his permanent home in the colonies, Lord Fairfax, settled near Frederick Town.

Nearby, an ambitious young Virginian by the name of George Washington purchased his first piece of land at Bullskin Creek. Washington defended the town during the majority of the French and Indian War, and one can still visit his office downtown. After the war and with the help of some spirituous inducements to aid in his election—a legal practice at the time—Washington won his first political office and represented the town and surrounding area in the House of Burgesses.

During the Civil War, the town hosted some of

Above: The Second Battle of Winchester, June 13-15, 1863, was an important Confederate victory and suggested that Lt. Gen. Richard Ewell would credibly succeed his recently deceased former commander, the fallen Stonewall Jackson. (dd/pg)

Opposite: The home Stonewall Jackson had used in Winchester as an office during the winter of 1861 and the spring of 1862, just prior to his famed Valley Campaign, belonged to Lt. Col. Lewis Tilghman Moore of the 31st Virginia Infantry. In 1960, with financial assistance from Moore's descendant, actress Mary Tyler Moore, the building opened as a museum. It claims to have "the largest collection of Jackson memorabilia and also personal objects from members of his staff." (cm)

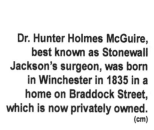

Dr. Hunter Holmes McGuire, best known as Stonewall Jackson's surgeon, was born in Winchester in 1835 in a home on Braddock Street, which is now privately owned. (cm)

the best-known military leaders of the conflict, including Confederate icon Thomas J. "Stonewall" Jackson. It also hosted some of the most notorious, including Union Gen. Robert Milroy, who attempted to bring the full force of the Emancipation Proclamation to bear on Winchester in early 1863.

War touched Winchester and left its mark. The city changed hands between North and South more than 70 times, including multiple times in a single day. Within the confines of the town, three major battles, all named Winchester, were fought in three successive years starting in 1862. To the immediate south, two more engagements at Kernstown in 1862 and 1864 brought the armies back to the area. The town courthouse was used as a hospital and a prison and sometimes both at the same time.

On September 19, 1864, the Confederate army was defeated at the third and final battle of Winchester and lost control of the town. Winchester would never change hands again. Union Gen. Philip Sheridan assigned Col. Oliver Edwards' brigade to garrison and provide provost marshal duties for Winchester. Put under martial law, Winchester was bleak that winter. The area suffered under severe weather and, with the destroyed gas works, was literally left in the dark. With a bored occupying force and desolate countryside, there was not much cheer as the calendar changed from 1864 to 1865.

On the night of April 9, 1865, Winchester residents were aroused with cannons booming and Union soldiers running gleefully through town shouting for joy. Bands added to the celebratory air. When curious citizens inquired the reason, they were told, "Lee surrendered." Pro-Southern citizens wondered what to expect next, and one recalled not "a word was spoken, but sobs were audible." This closed another chapter in the town's long history.

Country music legend Patsy Cline was born in Winchester in 1932. In 1963, at the age of 30, she died in a plane crash and was buried in Shenandoah Memorial Park. A bell tower tolls hymns daily at 6:00 p.m., the hour of Cline's death. (cm)

George Washington made his headquarters in Winchester
(above) from September 1755 through December of 1756 while
he oversaw construction of forts along the Virginia frontier,
including Fort Loudon at the north end of Winchester. Today,
Washington's office operates as a museum (right, top). (wrhs, cm)

The elegant Handley Library, located on West Piccadilly Street,
opened in 1913 after a $250,000 bequest from a judge from
Scranton, Pennsylvania (right, middle). (cm)

Abram's Delight is one of the oldest settlements in Winchester.
Established first as a log home in 1728, it became home to five
generations of Abraham Hollingsworth's family. A reproduction log
home sits on the site (right, bottom), along with the stone house
that replaced it. Abram's Delight, operated as a museum, is located
across from the Winchester-Frederick County Visitor Center. (cm)

Today, Winchester offers a wealth of American
history to see, including Jackson's Headquarters, the
Frederick County Historical Society, Washington's
Office, Shenandoah University, the Museum of the
Shenandoah Valley, and even the gravesite of country
music legend Patsy Cline. As one of the largest apple-
producing areas of the country, the town also hosts an
apple blossom festival every spring.

The town invites visitors to stay longer than the
soldiers of Nathaniel Bank's Union army in May 1862—
who, when asked, said they could not wait to "get back to
their own country!"

John Mosby, George Custer, and the Front Royal Executions

APPENDIX B

Two columns of gray riders cautiously approached the Federal ambulance train. Some moved their holsters around to the front of their belts, while others put wads of tobacco in their cheeks, anxiously awaiting the signal to attack. These men hailed from the 43rd Battalion of Virginia Cavalry, more popularly known as "Mosby's Rangers" after their commander, Col. John Singleton Mosby. For the upcoming assault, Capt. Walter Frankland's Rangers would strike the head of the train while Capt. Samuel Chapman would lead a contingent into its rear.

As Frankland sent his men forward, he could not have known the impact of his attack—or its consequences.

The Federals had set out just days earlier as part of Maj. Gen. Philip Sheridan's plan for assaulting the Confederate position on Fisher's Hill. Sheridan had assigned Maj. Gen. Alfred Torbert, his chief of cavalry, to lead the divisions of Brig. Gen. Wesley Merritt and Brig. Gen. James Wilson east into the adjoining Luray Valley. Torbert was then to ride south, reenter the Shenandoah Valley at New Market Gap, and trap the retreating Confederates.

The monument erected by Mosby's men in Prospect Hill Cemetery in Front Royal (left) served as much as a mark of defiance as of commemoration. (dd/pg)

Setting out on the morning of September 21, Merritt, less one brigade, rendezvoused with Wilson at the town of Front Royal. Wilson had engaged Brig. Gen. Williams C. Wickham's Confederate division. Finding that Wickham had abandoned his position, the Federal horsemen moved to overtake the Confederates the next morning. The Yankees advanced to Milford only to find the Rebels drawn up in a formidable position. After several hours of spirited skirmishing, Torbert called off the attack and began to withdraw.

Continuing their march through September 23, Merritt's division rode back to Front Royal. It was there Frankland's and Chapman's Rangers fell upon the column. In the ensuing attack, the Rangers found themselves outnumbered, and the Union horsemen quickly got the better of them. Scattering their foes in every direction, the Union troopers managed to capture six Rangers.

One of the Union wounded was Lt. Charles McMaster of the 2nd U.S. Cavalry.

Lieutenant Charles McMaster claimed he had surrendered to Confederates, who then shot him anyway. Confederates denied the allegation. The incident sparked a controversy that turned war personal. (wrhs)

Lieutenant McMaster was found by his comrades at the end of the fight, dismounted and shot through the head but still alive. The circumstances of McMaster's wounding were a subject of controversy. Although the Rangers denied the assertion, McMaster claimed he had been shot and left for dead after he had formally surrendered. This assertion did not take long to make the rounds.

Mosby's command was notorious for their guerrilla-style hit-and-run tactics. The Rangers routinely operated east of the Blue Ridge Mountains, in an area known as "Mosby's Confederacy." While moving through this area, no Federal supply train, picket post, or straggler was safe from Mosby's men. When the Valley campaign of 1864 opened, the Rangers moved to augment Lt. Gen. Jubal Early's army. Making their presence known on August 21, Mosby raided a wagon train at Berryville. The relentless raids and ambushes had worn down the nerves of the Federals. Word of McMaster's wounding after surrendering was too much to bear. The act must be avenged.

Torbert, Merritt, and George Custer were in Front Royal as the column filed into town. Also present was Col. Charles R. Lowell, McMaster's brigade commander.

At some point, someone from the officer pool sent word down the chain of command for the six captured Rangers to be executed.

David Jones and Lucien Love were taken behind the Methodist Church and shot. Henry Rhodes was 17, lived in the village, and had only ridden out to seek adventure with the Rangers that morning. He was taken to the Rose Hill farm and gunned down. Like Rhodes, the Union troopers took Thomas Anderson to the Criser farm and shot him. The final two captives, Thomas Overby and a man named Carter were hanged.

In the days following these ghastly events, John Mosby blamed George Custer. On November 6, Mosby retaliated. After capturing a number of men from Custer's division, Mosby ordered seven of them to hang near Rectortown. However, the executions were botched, and only three soldiers died.

In the postwar years, Mosby continued to blame Custer for the events at Front Royal. When his memoirs were published in 1917, well after Custer's death, Mosby still held him accountable. The damning evidence, according to Mosby, was that Custer did not mention the incident in his official report. His silence was implication enough.

However, available evidence suggests that the order to execute the Rangers came from Wesley Merritt, Custer's division commander. For Custer, then, it was impossible to explain in his official report an order that he never issued.

While Custer very well may have known of Mosby's charges, it is unclear whether he responded directly to them publicly. Despite the feelings of their chief, many of Mosby's Rangers accepted as truth that Custer did not order the executions.

On September 23, 1899, more than 200 Rangers returned to Front Royal to dedicate a monument to the men who were executed that day. The New York Times claimed that it was the largest gathering of Mosby's command since the end of the war. More than 5,000 individuals from as close as West Virginia and as far away as New York joined the veterans in remembering their comrades. The keynote address was delivered by one of the Rangers, Maj. Adolphus Richards. Interestingly enough, during the speech, Richards completely exonerated Custer of having any responsibility for the events that day.

Still standing in Prospect Hill Cemetery, the obelisk bears the names of those who died—a tribute of remembrance to one of the darkest hours of the nation's darkest years.

Union Brig. Gen. George Custer (top) and Confederate Col. John Mosby (bottom), two of the most romanticized figures of the war, clashed at the center of one of the great controversies of the 1864 Shenandoah Valley campaign. (loc)

Meadow Brook,
where Sheridan reunited
with his army (cm)

APPENDIX C
BY CHRIS MACKOWSKI
& PHILLIP S. GREENWALT

If the old saying is true about history being written by the victors, then Jubal A. Early is the exception that proves the rule. Inarguably, Early's postwar writings in defense of the Confederacy did more to influence ongoing interpretation of the Civil War than anything else. As a result, for a century and a half, many (if not most) Americans accepted Early's "Lost Cause" version of the war as fact. Confederates may have lost the Civil War, but Early helped them win the peace.

In that light, Phillip Sheridan's victory in the Shenandoah Valley in the autumn of 1864 is all the more impressive. Sheridan not only won the campaign—he trounced the man who, in essence, wrote the war's popular history.

"Trounced" isn't a stretch, either. Sheridan's manic twenty-mile ride from Winchester down to Cedar Creek on the morning of October 19 was immediately immortalized by Thomas Read, whose poem "Sheridan's Ride" quickly became a national sensation. "The first that the general saw were the groups/Of stragglers, and then the retreating troops;" Read wrote with cliffhanger drama and flourish:

What was done? what to do? a glance told him both,
Then, striking his spurs, with a terrible oath
He dashed down the line 'mid a storm of huzzas,
And the wave of retreat checked its course there, because
The sight of the master compelled it to pause.

Read, a prolific artist as well as writer, went on to paint a version of the scene in 1871 (which Sheridan and his horse posed for); that image still gets wide circulation in association with Cedar Creek.

President Lincoln's partisans circulated Read's poem widely in the lead-up to the November election as a reminder of the valiant Union victory. "Stick with us; we'll win this thing yet," the message suggested. Indeed, the entire incident could have been a metaphor for Lincoln's election: he very much hoped to snatch electoral victory from the jaws of what had looked like certain defeat earlier that summer.

Sheridan loved the attention that "Sheridan's Ride" garnered for him—so much so that he renamed his horse, from "Rienzi" to "Winchester," in honor of the episode.

He even had the hide of his horse mounted after it died, and then had the taxidermical masterpiece put on

public display. To this day, the mounted hide of the horse stands on display in the Smithsonian's Museum of American History.

There is no doubt that Sheridan, when he splashed across Meadow Brook, provided inspiration to the flagging spirits of the Union army. But the army he rallied was hardly defeated. They had received the best the Confederates could offer and been pushed back, but by the time Sheridan swept in, the army had already rallied and stabilized its defenses.

Sheridan's own writings suggested otherwise, though. He wrote in his official report of his efforts to "stem the torrent of fugitives." He was "happy to say that hundreds of the men, when reflection found they had not done themselves justice, came back with cheers."

So the story went, and so it grew. For instance, Brig. Gen. G. W. Forsyth, an aide-de-camp who'd accompanied Sheridan on the ride, described the event in even more hyperbolic fashion in an article for *Scribner's* that he later included in his memoir, *Thrilling Days in Army Life*, published in 1900. "As we debouched into the fields," he wrote of the climactic moment,

Following his well-publicized poem done a mere two weeks after the ride, Thomas Read six years later portrayed Sheridan's Ride with oil on canvas (above). An 1886 facsimile by Louis Prang and Company was based on Read's famous painting (below). (loc)

> *the general would wave his hat to the men and point to the front, never lessening his speed as he pressed forward. It was enough. One glance at the eager face*

and familiar black horse and they knew him and,
starting to their feet, they swung their caps around their
heads and broke into cheers as he passed beyond them;
and then gathering up their belongings started after him
for the front, shouting to their comrades farther out in
the fields, "Sheridan! Sheridan!"

One might suggest that Sheridan's version of events stuck as it did because, after all, he eventually rose to become general-in-chief of the entire army. As his fame and success grew after the war, so too did the image of him riding along the Valley Turnpike to rally his broken army.

However, one need only look at Sheridan's boss, Ulysses S. Grant, to understand that office alone cannot ensure one's version of history will stick. Grant's rank, his eventual rise to the presidency, his ongoing adoration by veterans, and his authorship of his *Personal Memoirs*— a literary masterwork—all paled in the longevity of their power when compared to the unrelenting literary onslaught of Early and his fellow Lost Cause writers.

"Clear-eyed in his determination to sway future generations, Early used his own writings and his influence with other ex-Confederates to foster a heroic image of Robert E. Lee and the Southern war effort," says historian Gary Gallagher, who has extensively studied Early's writings and their impact. "Many of the ideas these men articulated became orthodoxy in the postwar South, eventually made their way into the broader national perception of the war, and remain vigorous today."

Ironically, it was a war of words with Sheridan over the Valley Campaign's casualty figures that sparked Early's attempts to chronicle—and thus interpret— the war. As the two antagonists refought the campaign through newspaper articles, Early refuted Sheridan's claims about the "great slaughter" of the Confederate force at Cedar Creek. Early pointed to Sheridan's exaggerations as self-aggrandizing proof that the Union general could not be trusted, and he called on "all fair minded men of other nations to withhold their judgment . . . until the truth can be placed before them."

Ulysses S. Grant, in his Personal Memoirs, made the boldly erroneous assertion that "Early had lost more

"As [Sheridan] met the fugitives he ordered them to turn back, reminding them that they were going the wrong way. His presence soon restored confidence. Finding themselves worse frightened than hurt the men did halt and turn back. Many of those who had run ten miles got back in time to redeem their reputations as gallant soldiers before night."

—*from The Personal Memoirs of Ulysses S. Grant*

men in killed, wounded and captured in the [V]alley than Sheridan had commanded from first to last"—a statement that, if true, would have meant Early vastly outnumbered Sheridan (which, of course, he didn't). Early jumped on Grant the same way he jumped on Sheridan, blasting "the recklessness of these statements."

It must have rankled Early, proudly unreconstructed as he was after the war, to see his former Valley opponent propelled to such lofty heights. "If Sheridan had not had subordinates of more ability and energy than himself, I should probably have had to write a different history of my Valley campaign," Early scoffed.

The story Early did write managed to sustain the honor of "hopelessly outnumbered Confederates," says Gallagher, and thus "cast his own performance in a better light." Yet he could not erase the stain of defeat. As a result, his larger postwar attempts to recast events in the Valley to his favor proved for naught.

While a historical marker along the Valley Pike indicates the area of Sheridan's return, the actual location is off the road about a half a mile away along Meadow Brook. (cm)

It could be that Early had not only Sheridan to contend with but a figure of even greater magnitude: the nearly mythic stature of Stonewall Jackson, whose exploits in the Valley in the spring of 1862 had propelled him to international fame. At a time when the Confederacy's fortunes had been on the decline nearly everywhere else, Jackson's victories proved a much-needed bright spot for people of Southern sympathies. By the autumn of 1864, eighteen months after his death, Jackson had already risen to the position of Confederate martyr. Early had no way to compete.

"General Jackson did not have the odds opposed to him which I had, and his troops were composed entirely of the very best material which entered into the composition of our armies," Early later said, admitting that many of those same units served under his command but had also, after two years' time, nearly

Described in Thomas Reed's poem as "A steed as black as the steeds of night," Sheridan's horse, Rienzi, became almost as famous as his owner. Rienzi was a black gelding who measured nearly seventeen hands high. Sheridan called him "an animal of great intelligence and immense strength and endurance. He always held his head high, and by the quickness of his movements gave many persons the idea that he was exceedingly impetuous. This was not so, for I could at any time control him by a firm hand

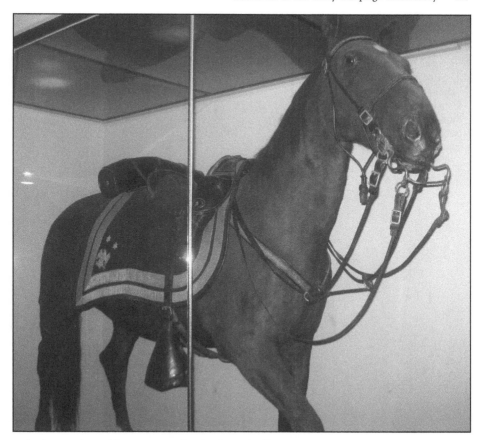

and a few words, and he was as cool and quiet under fire as one of my soldiers." Rienzi was given to Sheridan in 1862 by officers of the 2nd Michigan Cavalry when the regiment was stationed in Rienzi, Mississippi, and Sheridan used him for the remainder of the war, including during his ascent up Missonary Ridge during the battles for Chattanooga in November of 1863 and his line-breaking charge at Five Forks in April of 1865. Rienzi was wounded several times in action but survived the war. He eventually died in Chicago in 1878.

Sheridan admired the horse so much that he asked a taxidermist to mount the hide for public display, and for years it stood at the military museum at Governor's Island in New York. When the museum burned in 1922, Rienzi survived, and under escort from an army honor guard, the horse was transferred to the Smithsonian Institution, where it remains on display in the Museum of American History. The saddle, bridle, blanket, and other tack he still wears all belonged to Sheridan.

Rienzi is one of only eight mounted horses in the world and one of only two Civil War horses; the other Civil War horse is Stonewall Jackson's "Little Sorrel" on display at V.M.I. Also in the "mounted mounts" club: Roy Rogers' and Dale Evans's Trigger and Buttermilk, on display at the Roy Rogers Museum in Branson, Missouri; Marengo, one of Napoleon's horses, on display in England's National Army Museum; Phar Lap, Australia's most famous race horse, on display at the Museum of Victoria; and Comanche, a horse who had belonged to one of Gen. George Armstrong Custer's officers and was the only survivor of Custer's Last Stand at Little Big Horn, on display at the University of Kansas. Old Baldy, Union General George Meade's horse, almost makes it into the club by a nose; his mounted head hangs on a plaque on display at the Grand Army of the Republic Museum in Philadelphia. (loc/cm)

Harper's Weekly depicted "Sheridan's Ride" on the cover of its November 5, 1864, edition. Ironically, at least for Jubal Early, the sketch of Sheridan bore a striking resemblance to Stonewall Jackson, complete with slouch hat. Early would lose the battle for memory in the Valley to both men. (sos)

expended themselves. "Besides the old soldiers whose numbers were so reduced, my command was composed of recruits and conscripts."

Early also bemoaned the disadvantages Sheridan's Burning inflicted on his army. "The Valley, at the time of [Jackson's] campaign, was teeming with provisions, and forage from one end to the other," Early wrote; "while my command had very great difficulty in obtaining provisions for the men, and had to rely almost entirely on the grass in the open fields for forage."

Early went on to offer other defenses, most of which were legitimate albeit tinged with the defensiveness of a self-apologist. "These facts do not detract from the merits of General Jackson's campaign in the slightest degree, and far be it from me to attempt to obscure his well earned and richly deserved fame," he concluded. "They only show that I ought not to be condemned for not doing what he did."

Despite Early's disdain for Sheridan, the bandy-legged Irishman proved a far more capable foe for Early than anyone Jackson had contended with. In the spring of 1862, losers like Milroy, Shields, and Banks had yet to be culled from the ranks of general officers or shuffled off to less important (that is, politically visible) theaters of the war. Jackson's audacity certainly played a role in his string of victories in the spring of 1862, but so, too, did the B-list nature of his adversaries. Early. in contrast, was up against one of Grant's favored sons.

In the long run, Early was also up against himself.

With Kristopher D. White, Chris Mackowski is the co-founder of Emerging Civil War and managing editor of the Emerging Civil War Series. Dr. Mackowski is a professor of journalism and mass communication at St. Bonaventure University.

The mythmaking he'd begun with the Lost Cause put primacy on the war in the Eastern Theater (since, after all, Confederates kept getting drubbed in the West). In the East-centric narrative, the "noble Lee" stands at the center of the story, with the martyred Jackson by his side (at least through May of 1863). By necessity, that puts primacy on the Washington-Richmond axis of action at the expense of action in the Valley. The Valley is useful to that narrative only in that it helps build Jackson into the genius so important as Lee's right hand. In order to promote his own vision of history, Early essentially had to write himself out of the main storyline.

Battered not only by Sheridan but by Jackson's memory, it's little wonder Early lost the Valley Campaign in all respects. What's become even more ironic, though, is that the iconic story of Sheridan's Ride—like the Lost Cause itself—has overshadowed the actual history.

Sheridan not only beat Early on the battlefield; wittingly or not, he beat Early at his own game.

After Lee's surrender of Lee, Early went west of the Mississippi River looking for any Confederate force still fighting. After discovering they'd all surrendered, Early went abroad rather than live in the reconstructed South. Pardoned in 1868, though, he returned to Virginia to practice law and vigorously defend the South's actions during the war. In doing so, he did much to shape the "Lost Cause" symbolism of the defeated Confederacy. After a fall down the steps, Early died the next day on March 2, 1894. He was buried in Spring Hill Cemetery in Lynchburg, Virginia. (pg)

Sheridan's Ride
BY THOMAS BUCHANAN READ (1864)

Up from the South at break of day,
Bringing to Winchester fresh dismay,
The affrighted air with a shudder bore,
Like a herald in haste, to the chieftain's door,
The terrible grumble, and rumble, and roar,
Telling the battle was on once more,
And Sheridan twenty miles away.

And wider still those billows of war,
Thundered along the horizon's bar;
And louder yet into Winchester rolled
The roar of that red sea uncontrolled,
Making the blood of the listener cold,
As he thought of the stake in that fiery fray,
And Sheridan twenty miles away.

But there is a road from Winchester town,
A good, broad highway leading down;
And there, through the flush of the morning light,
A steed as black as the steeds of night,
Was seen to pass, as with eagle flight,
As if he knew the terrible need;
He stretched away with his utmost speed;
Hills rose and fell; but his heart was gay,
With Sheridan fifteen miles away.

cont. next page

Still sprung from those swift hoofs, thundering South,
The dust, like smoke from the cannon's mouth;
Or the trail of a comet, sweeping faster and faster,
Foreboding to traitors the doom of disaster.
The heart of the steed, and the heart of the master
Were beating like prisoners assaulting their walls,
Impatient to be where the battle-field calls;
Every nerve of the charger was strained to full play,
With Sheridan only ten miles away.

Under his spurning feet the road
Like an arrowy Alpine river flowed,
And the landscape sped away behind
Like an ocean flying before the wind,
And the steed, like a barque fed with furnace ire,
Swept on, with his wild eyes full of fire.
But lo! he is nearing his heart's desire;
He is snuffing the smoke of the roaring fray,
With Sheridan only five miles away.

The first that the general saw were the groups
Of stragglers, and then the retreating troops;
What was done? what to do? a glance told him both,
Then, striking his spurs, with a terrible oath,
He dashed down the line 'mid a storm of huzzas,
And the wave of retreat checked its course there, because
The sight of the master compelled it to pause.
With foam and with dust the black charger was gray;
By the flash of his eye, and the red nostril's play,
He seemed to the whole great army to say,
"I have brought you Sheridan all the way
From Winchester, down to save the day!"

Hurrah! hurrah for Sheridan!
Hurrah! hurrah for horse and man!
And when their statues are placed on high,
Under the dome of the Union sky,
The American soldier's Temple of Fame;
There with the glorious general's name,
Be it said, in letters both bold and bright,
   "Here is the steed that saved the day,
By carrying Sheridan into the fight,
   From Winchester, twenty miles away!"

Right: Several composers put Read's poem to music. (loc)

Opposite: An equestrian statue of Sheridan and Rienzi sits in Washington, D.C.'s Sheridan Circle, along Massachusetts Ave. near Embassy Row. The statue was sculpted by Gutzon Borglum, the artist who later did Mt. Rushmore in South Dakota and Stone Mountain in Georgia. Borglum earned the commission after winning a competition in 1908. A duplicate was erected in Chicago, where Sheridan had lived, in 1923. (dd)

Preserving the Shenandoah Valley's Civil War Battlefields

APPENDIX D
BY ERIC CAMPBELL
Park Ranger, Cedar Creek and
Belle Grove National Historical Park

In many parts of the [Shenandoah] Valley, the 19th century lies close to the surface with merely a veneer of changes. The land is farmed, as it was a hundred years ago. Old houses, mills, and churches survive, or their foundations may be located. The new road network is congruent with the old. Paved county roads follow the winding courses of old farm roads. Small villages have grown into larger towns, yet preserve their core as a historic district. Most importantly, the scenic beauty of the Blue Ridge, North Mountain, and the Shenandoah River continues to enhance the quality of life of Valley residents and to attract hundreds of thousands of visitors per year. When one knows where to look, the Civil War history of the Shenandoah Valley is everywhere.

("Study of Civil War Sites in the Shenandoah Valley" Public Law 101-628)

The story of preservation of Civil War sites and battlefields in Virginia's Shenandoah Valley is, in many ways, the story of the modern preservation movement. While famous battlefields such as Gettysburg, Vicksburg, Chickamauga, and Chattanooga, among others, were preserved by the federal government during the lifetimes of the Union and Confederate soldiers who fought there—in the late 19th and early 20th centuries—Civil War sites in the Shenandoah Valley were largely ignored.

It was not until a hundred years later, around the time of the centennial commemoration of the war in the 1960s, that the first preservation efforts began in the Valley when the Virginia Military Institute purchased 200 acres of the New Market battlefield (less than 10 percent of the "core battlefield"). A few years later, in 1969, Edwin Bearss, chief historian of the National Park Service, and historian John D. McDermott submitted the Belle Grove Manor house and the Cedar Creek battlefield for the National Register of Historic Places. Though these were significant steps, it still left nearly all of the Valley's battlefields in private hands and wholly unprotected.

Despite this, threats to these battlefields remained rather low, as the Shenandoah Valley retained its rural character. Farming continued as the primary economic activity in the Valley well into the mid-20th century, and although farming technology improved, residents used the land much as their predecessors did—to grow crops and raise livestock.

A plaque outside Belle Grove, erected in November of 2008, reads: "This incomparable view preserved by....." (cm)

All of this changed dramatically in the 1960s, beginning with the construction of the interstate highway system. Interstate 81, which runs the length of the Valley paralleling the old Valley Turnpike (US Route 11), was the single most destructive event to the area's battlefields, cutting through 11 different sites (First, Second, and Third Winchester, Rutherford's farm, Second Kernstown, Cedar Creek, Fisher's Hill, Tom's Brook, and New Market). The physical damage of these interstates was subsequently compounded during the decades since by associated development.

As an example, large tracts of the Cedar Creek battlefield were slated for commercial development in the 1980s. This threat led directly to the creation of the Cedar Creek Battlefield Foundation (CCBF) in 1987. This grassroots effort involved concerned local citizens who banded together in order to save these parcels. Today, CCBF preserves more than 300 acres of core battlefield land at Cedar Creek.

It was at this same time that a "perfect storm" of events occurred which resulted in the beginnings of the modern Civil War preservation movement. This included the 125th anniversary commemoration of the war (1986-1990), which renewed interest in the conflict among the general public, combined with significant threats to, if not outright destruction of, several battlefields, including Manassas and Chantilly respectively. Not surprisingly, the battlefields of the Shenandoah Valley were tightly linked to this resurgence to save America's hallowed ground.

One result of the public outcry to these threatened battlefields was a Congressionally-mandated 1990 "Study of Civil War Sites in the Shenandoah Valley" (Public Law 101-628). This study, the first of its kind, was to

identify significant Civil War sites in the Shenandoah Valley, to determine their condition, to establish their

Built circa 1800, the Heater House sits in the middle of the Cedar Creek battlefield (in the photo below, to the right). Mrs. Heater, a native of Pennsylvania, remained a Unionist during the war although she had two sons die in Confederate service. In the 1980s, the 600-acre farm was eyed for commercial development, but the work of preservationists saved some 300 acres of core battlefield. (cm)

relative importance, to assess short- and long-term threats to their integrity, and to provide alternatives for their preservation and interpretation.

The report studied 15 battlefields (Front Royal, First Winchester, Second Winchester, Third Winchester, New Market, First Kernstown, Second Kernstown, Tom's Brook, Cool Spring, Fisher's Hill, Cedar Creek, Cross Keys, Port Republic, Piedmont, and McDowell) and was delivered to the Secretary of the Interior and Congress in September 1992. (A 2012 update to this study added the battlefields of Rutherford's Farm, Guard Hill, Manassas Gap, Waynesboro and Berryville).

As this landmark study was underway, and as a direct off-shoot of it, a far more encompassing government program was established in 1991 to review the condition and preservation of all Civil War battlefields nationwide. The Civil War Sites Advisory Commission (CWSAC) was tasked with undertaking

a two-year study that identified the nation's historically significant Civil War battlefields, determined their relative importance and their current condition, assessed threats to their integrity, and recommended alternatives for preserving and interpreting them.

When this report was presented to Congress in 1993, one of its recommendations was the creation of the American Battlefield Protection Program (ABPP). The ABPP is one of the incredible success stories of the modern preservation movement. This government agency, a part of the National Park Service, "promotes the preservation of significant historic battlefields associated with wars on American soil" by providing technical assistance for preservation, management, and interpretation issues; raising public awareness; and overseeing the issuing of millions of dollars in federal grants to non-federal, mostly nonprofit organizations, to preserve tens of thousands of battlefield acreage across the country.

The CWSAC also surveyed and rated 384 of the nation's battlefields on not only their military importance (Class A, "having a decisive influence on a campaign and a direct impact on the course of the war," through Class D, "having a limited influence on the outcome of a campaign . . . but . . . affecting local objectives"), but also on "military, economic, and social significance and the exceptional interpretive potential that each site might have." Thus factors such as total casualties, loss of a significant military figure, important lessons in strategy or tactics, unusual importance of the battle in the public mind, effect on national politics, involvement of minority troops, high archeological potential, and interpretive potential were used to create these rankings.

The CWSAC report ranked more than half (twelve) of the Shenandoah Valley battlefields as either Class A (First Winchester, Third Winchester, and Cedar Creek) or Class B (First Kernstown, Second Kernstown, Second Winchester, Fisher's Hill, Cross Keys, Port Republic, New Market, Piedmont, and Waynesboro). Six more were ranked as Class C (Cool Spring, Guard Hill, Berryville, Tom's Brook, McDowell, and Front Royal). Only two were classified as Class D (Rutherford's Farm and Manassas Gap). Thus it was obvious: these fields had a significant influence on the outcome of the war, both on a national and regional level.

But changes to the Valley's rural character had already taken a toll. The 1990s Shenandoah Valley Study rated four of the 15 battlefields as being in "Good" condition (McDowell, Cross Keys, Piedmont, and Port Republic). Four others were rated as "Fair" (Cool Spring, Fisher's Hill, Tom's Brook, and Cedar Creek), and five were found to be in "Poor" condition (First and Second Kernstown, Second Winchester, New Market, and Front Royal). Only the First Winchester battlefield was deemed to be "Lost."

In the more than 20 years since these two studies were completed, preservation of Civil War sites in the Shenandoah Valley has experienced both resounding success and frustrating failure.

Two major recommendations made in the Shenandoah Valley Study have both come to fruition. The first was the creation of a national heritage area or cultural corridor in the Valley. The Shenandoah Valley Battlefields National Historic District (SVBNHD) was created by Congress in 1996, and is now managed by the Shenandoah Valley Battlefields Foundation (SVBF). The foundation works with national, state, and regional organizations, along with private landowners, to coordinate the preservation, management, and interpretation of all Civil War sites. The SVBNHD is the only national heritage area or historic district in the country authorized by Congress to actually purchase and manage land. The SVBF has directly preserved, through either outright purchase or through easements, nearly 3,000 acres on 10 Valley battlefields (including Cedar Creek, Second and Third Winchester, Fisher's Hill, Tom's Brook, McDowell, Cross Keys, and Port Republic). It has also assisted various national and state organizations, along with nonprofit groups, to save almost 4,000 additional acres. This represents nearly a quarter of the core land on these battlefields. This includes nearly 500 acres at Cedar Creek, making the foundation the largest owner of preserved land on that battlefield.

Three of most significant projects the foundation has recently undertaken involve Third Winchester (where more than 610 contiguous acres of the field are now preserved and progress is well underway to create infrastructure and interpretive media, such as visitor facilities, trails, signage, brochures and maps, and battlefield restoration); the Fisher's Hill Trail project (a multi-year project to create a five-mile long visitor use trail that will connect the battlefield to Strasburg and the Cedar Creek battlefield beyond); and Star Fort (where this long-neglected Civil War fortification has been restored and opened to the public, with trails and

Fisher's Hill remains protected largely through the efforts of the American Battlefield Trust, which preserved more than 360 acres. (cm)

interpretive signage). The foundation has also done much to establish and promote Civil War heritage tourism in throughout Valley.

The second major recommendation of the 1990 Study was the creation of a national park service unit in the Valley. Cedar Creek and Belle Grove National Historical Park was authorized by Congress in 2002. This unique park is based on a partnership model, where the National Park Service works with several nonprofit organizations to preserve and interpret the history of the Shenandoah Valley, from its earliest creation through the Civil War. The organizations, all of whom were involved in the preservation of the Cedar Creek battlefield prior to the creation of the park itself, include The National Trust for Historic Preservation; Belle Grove, Inc.; the Cedar Creek Battlefield Foundation; the Shenandoah Valley Battlefields Foundation; and Shenandoah County. Together, these organizations, along with the National Park Service, have

Creation of the Shenandoah Battlefields National Historic District in 1996 did much to draw attention to the Valley's key role in the Civil War. The district covers eight counties and stretches from Winchester in the north to Staunton in the south. It encompasses actions associated with both the 1862 and 1864 Valley campaigns, Lee's march to Gettysburg, and the battle of New Market. (cm)

preserved more than 1,500 acres of the battlefield (just less than half of the 3,700 acres within the park's authorized boundary). This includes, among many resources, Belle Grove (a 1790s plantation manor house), Harmony Hall (an 18th century settlement house), the Heater house (an historic witness structure), Civil War entrenchments built by the Union VIII and XIX corps prior to the battle, and the Bowman-Hite house (a 1840s witness structure). The National Park Service began interpretive operations in 2010 and opened a visitor contact station in 2013 with exhibits and displays, including a fiber optic map explaining the battle.

Other success stories in the Valley include the preservation of significant portions of the First and Second Kernstown battlefields (through the efforts of the Kernstown Battlefield Association, a grassroots nonprofit organization created by local concerned citizens and the Museum of the Shenandoah Valley, which owns the historic Rose Hill farm at First Kernstown); 1,200 contiguous acres preserved at McDowell (by the Lee-Jackson Education Association, American Battlefield Trust, and SVBF); 648 acres at Tom's Brook (by SVBF and the American Battlefield Trust); nearly 600 acres at New Market (New Market Battlefield State Park and SVBF); the purchase in 2012 of 77 acres at Cedar Creek

*A 28-year National Park Service veteran,
Eric Campbell has served as a ranger-historian at Cedar Creek and Belle Grove National Historical Park since 2009, where he has overseen the planning and creation of the park's interpretation.*

(by the National Park Service and American Battlefield Trust, and includes the 8th Vermont monument, one of only three veteran memorials on the battlefield); and the 2013 public-private partnership between the American Battlefield Trust and Shenandoah University to protect 195 acres of the Cool Spring battlefield.

However, there have also been failures throughout the years, and significant threats remain. One of the most unfortunate was the recent loss of a large section of the Rutherford's Farm battlefield to commercial development. Some of the most significant threats include the proposed widening of Interstate 81 throughout the length of the Valley, which would destroy thousands of acres of core battlefield land (including nearly 450 acres at Cedar Creek alone), the expansion of an industrial limestone quarry on the Cedar Creek battlefield (which is already ongoing and will eventually destroy 450 acres of core battlefield land), and the constantly encroaching residential and commercial development, which swallows thousands of acres of Valley farmland (among them battlefields) each year.

Clearly, the future of these critical battlefield resources in the Shenandoah Valley is at a crossroads. While significant progress has been made in the last two decades, with nearly 7,000 acres of core battlefield preserved, much work still remains. According the latest calculations by the Shenandoah Valley Battlefields Foundation, there are "still more than 13,815 acres of core battlefield land at our primary sites that are unprotected but retain the integrity needed to convey the Valley's Civil War story."

Of course the more important point is that the Valley will continue to change and evolve. In the age of shrinking federal and state budgets, there are always fewer funds available for preservation purposes. Saving as much of these fields as possible before time runs out is critical. Although written more than 20 years ago, the following passage of the 1990 Shenandoah Valley Civil War Study is just as poignant today:

The history of the Civil War in the Shenandoah Valley bears witness to the devastation and waste of warfare, but more importantly, it underscores the irrepressible human will to survive, to rebuild, to carry on. Lessons which will continue to have relevance for generations to come. The historic events and the human players of the Valley—the heroic and the tragic alike--have contributed significantly to the texture of our American cultural heritage.

Certainly, these battlefields are worth saving.

TO HELP, CONTACT:

**Shenandoah Valley
Battlefields Foundation
PO Box 897
New Market, Virginia 22844
(540) 740-4545
www.shenandoahatwar.org**

**American Battlefield Trust
1156 15th Street NW, Suite 900
Washington, DC 20005
(202) 367-1861
www.battlefields.org**

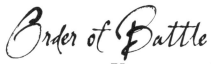

THE SHENANDOAH VALLEY CAMPAIGN OF 1864

ARMY OF THE SHENANDOAH Maj. Gen. Philip Sheridan

Escort *6th Pennsylvania Cavalry • 17th Pennsylvania Cavalry (detachment)*

VI CORPS Maj. Gen. Horatio Wright, Brig. Gen. James Ricketts, Brig. Gen. George Getty
First Division Brig. Gen. David Russell (k), Brig. Gen. Frank Wheaton
First Brigade Lt. Col. Edward Campbell (w), Lt. Col. Edward Penrose (w)
4th New Jersey • 10th New Jersey • 15th New Jersey

Second Brigade Brig. Gen. Emory Upton (w), Col. Joseph Hamblin (w),
Col. Ranald MacKenzie (w), Lt. Col. Egbert Olcott
2nd Connecticut Heavy Artillery • 65th New York • 121st New York • 95th Pennsylvania • 96th Pennsylvania

Third Brigade Col. Oliver Edwards
37th Massachusetts • 49th Pennsylvania • 82nd Pennsylvania • 119th Pennsylvania
2nd Rhode Island (battalion) • 5th Wisconsin (battalion)

Second Division Brig. Gen. George Getty, Brig. Gen. Lewis Grant
First Brigade Brig. Gen. Frank Wheaton, Col. James Warner
62nd New York • 93rd Pennsylvania • 98th Pennsylvania • 102nd Pennsylvania • 139th Pennsylvania

Second Brigade Col. James M. Warner, Col. George Foster, Brig. Gen. Lewis Grant
2nd Vermont • 3rd Vermont • 4th Vermont • 5th Vermont • 6th Vermont • 1st Vermont Heavy Artillery

Third Brigade Brig. Gen. Daniel D. Bidwell (k), Lt. Col. Winsor French
7th Maine • 43rd New York • 77th New York • 122nd New York • 49th New York (battalion)
61st Pennsylvania (battalion)

Third Division Brig. Gen. James Ricketts (w), Col. J. Warren Keifer
First Brigade Col. William Emerson
14th New Jersey • 106th New York • 151st New York • 87th Pennsylvania • 10th Vermont
184th New York (battalion)

Second Brigade Col. J. Warren Keifer, Col. William Ball
6th Maryland • 9th New York Heavy Infantry • 110th Ohio • 122nd Ohio • 126th Ohio
67th Pennsylvania • 138th Pennsylvania

Artillery Brigade Col. Charles H. Tompkins
Battery E, 5th Maine • 1st New York Light • Battery C, 1st Rhode Island • Battery G, 1st Rhode Island
Battery M, 5th United States

XIX CORPS Maj. Gen. William Emory
First Division Brig. Gen. William Dwight, Brig. Gen. James McMillan
First Brigade Col. George Beal, Col. Edwin Davis
29th Maine • 30th Massachusetts • 90th New York • 114th New York • 116th New York • 153rd New York

Second Brigade Brig. Gen. James W. McMillan, Col. Stephen Thomas
12th Connecticut • 160th New York • 47th Pennsylvania • 8th Vermont

Third Brigade Col. Leonard D. H. Currie
30th Maine • 133rd New York • 162nd New York • 165th New York (6 companies) • 173rd New York

Artillery *5th New York Light*

Second Division Brig. Gen. Cuvier Grover (w), Brig. Gen. Henry W. Birge
First Brigade Brig. Gen. Henry Birge, Col. Thomas W. Porter
9th Connecticut • 12th Maine • 14th Maine • 26th Massachusetts • 14th New Hampshire • 75th New York

Second Brigade Col. Edward L. Molineux
13th Connecticut • 11th Indiana • 22nd Iowa • 3rd Massachusetts Cavalry (dismounted) • 131st New York
159th New York

Third Brigade Col. Jacob Sharpe (w), Lt. Col. Alfred Neafie, Col. Daniel Macauley (w)
38th Massachusetts • 128th New York • 156th New York • 176th New York • 175th New York (battalion)

Fourth Brigade Col. David Shunk
8th Indiana • 18th Indiana • 24th Iowa • 28th Iowa

Artillery *Battery A, 1st Maine Light*

Reserve Artillery Capt. Elijah Taft, Maj. Albert W. Bradbury
17th Indiana Light • Battery D, 1st Rhode Island Light

ARMY OF WEST VIRGINIA Maj. Gen. George Crook
First Division Col. Joseph Thoburn (k)
First Brigade Col. George Wells (k), Lt. Col. Thomas Wildes
34th Massachusetts • 116th Ohio • 123rd Ohio • 5th New York Heavy Artillery (2nd Battalion)

Second Brigade Lt. Col. Robert S. Northcott, Col. William Curtis
1st West Virginia • 4th West Virginia • 12th West Virginia

Third Brigade Col. Thomas Harris, Col. Milton Wells
54th Pennsylvania • 10th West Virginia • 11th West Virginia • 15th West Virginia • 23rd Illinois Battalion

Second Division Col. Isaac Duval (w), Col. Rutherford B. Hayes
First Brigade Col. Rutherford B. Hayes, Col. Hiram Devol
23rd Ohio • 36th Ohio • 13th West Virginia • 5th West Virginia Battalion

Second Brigade Col. Daniel Johnson, Col. Benjamin Coates
91st Ohio • 9th West Virginia • 14th West Virginia • 34th Ohio Battalion

Artillery Brigade Capt. Henry Dupont
Battery L, 1st Ohio Light • Battery D, 1st Pennsylvania Light • Battery B, 5th United States

CAVALRY CORPS Bvt. Maj. Gen. Alfred T. A. Torbert
Escort *1st Rhode Island*

First Division Brig. Gen. Wesley Merritt
First Brigade Brig. Gen. George A. Custer, Col. James Kidd
1st Michigan • 5th Michigan • 6th Michigan • 7th Michigan • 25th New York

Second Brigade Col. Thomas C. Devin
4th New York • 6th New York • 9th New York • 19th New York (1st Dragoons) • 17th Pennsylvania

Reserve Brigade Col. Charles R. Lowell, Jr. (k), Lt. Col. Caspar Crowninshield
2nd Massachusetts • 6th Pennsylvania • 1st United States • 2nd United States • 5th United States

Artillery *6th New York Light • Batteries K & L, 1st United States*

Second Division Brig. Gen. William Averell, Col. William Powell
First Brigade Col. James N. Schoonmaker, Col. Alpheus S. Moore
8th Ohio (detachment) • 14th Pennsylvania • 22nd Pennsylvania

Second Brigade Col. Henry Capehart
1st New York • 1st West Virginia • 2nd West Virginia • 3rd West Virginia

Artillery *Battery L, 5th United States*

Third Division Brig. Gen. James Wilson
First Brigade Brig. Gen. John B. McIntosh (w), Col. George M. Purington, Col. Alexander Pennington
1st Connecticut • 3rd New Jersey • 2nd New York • 5th New York • 2nd Ohio • 18th Pennsylvania

Second Brigade Brig. Gen. George Chapman, Col. William Wells
3rd Indiana (2 companies) • 8th New York • 22nd New York • 1st Vermont • 1st New Hampshire (battalion)

Artillery *Batteries B & L, 2nd United States, Batteries C, F, & K, 3rd United States*

Provisional Division J. Howard Kitching (mw)
Made up of smaller detachments of infantry from each corps and Army of West Virginia. Only 6th New York Heavy Artillery saw action at Cedar Creek.

* * *

ARMY OF THE VALLEY Lt. Gen. Jubal A. Early
Major General John Breckinridge commanded Gordon's and Wharton's division until his transfer after Third Winchester.

Second Corps Maj. Gen. John B. Gordon
Rodes' Division Maj. Gen. Robert E. Rodes (k)[1], Maj. Gen. Stephen D. Ramseur (mw)[2]
Battle's Brigade Brig. Gen. Cullen A. Battle (w)[3], Lt. Col. Edwin L. Hobson
3rd Alabama • 5th Alabama • 6th Alabama • 12th Alabama • 61st Alabama

Grimes' Brigade Brig. Gen. Bryan Grimes
32nd North Carolina • 43rd North Carolina • 45th North Carolina • 53rd North Carolina • 2nd North Carolina Battalion

Cook's Brigade Brig. Gen. Philip Cook
4th Georgia • 12th Georgia • 21st Georgia • 44th Georgia

Cox's Brigade Brig. Gen. William R. Cox
*1st North Carolina • 2nd North Carolina • 3rd North Carolina • 4th North Carolina
14th North Carolina • 30th North Carolina*

Ramseur's Division Maj. Gen. Stephen D. Ramseur (k)[4], Brig. Gen. John Pegram
Pegram's Brigade Brig. Gen. John Pegram, Col. John S. Hoffman
13th Virginia • 31st Virginia • 49th Virginia • 52nd Virginia • 58th Virginia

Johnston's Brigade Brig. Gen. Robert D. Johnston (w)[5]
*5th North Carolina • 12th North Carolina • 20th North Carolina • 23rd North Carolina
1st North Carolina Battalion Sharpshooters*

Godwin's Brigade Brig. Gen. Archibald C. Godwin (k)[6], Lt. Col. William S. Davis
6th North Carolina • 21st North Carolina • 54th North Carolina • 57th North Carolina

Gordon's Division Maj. Gen. John B. Gordon[7], Brig. Gen. Clement A. Evans
Evans' Brigade Brig. Gen. Clement A. Evans, Col. Edmund N. Atkinson[8], Col. John H. Lowe
13th Georgia • 26th Georgia • 31st Georgia • 38th Georgia • 60th Georgia • 61st Georgia • 12th Georgia Battalion

Terry's Brigade Brig. Gen. William Terry[9]
*2nd Virginia • 4th Virginia • 5th Virginia • 10th Virginia • 21st Virginia • 23rd Virginia • 25th Virginia
27th Virginia • 33rd Virginia • 37th Virginia • 42nd Virginia • 44th Virginia • 48th Virginia • 50th Virginia*

York's Brigade Brig. Gen. Zebulon York (w)[10], Col. Edmund Pendleton
*1st Louisiana • 2nd Louisiana • 5th Louisiana • 6th Louisiana • 7th Louisiana • 8th Louisiana
9th Louisiana • 10th Louisiana • 14th Louisiana • 15th Louisiana*

Wharton's Division Brig. Gen. Gabriel C. Wharton
Wharton's Brigade Col. Augustus Forsberg (w)[11] Capt. Robert H. Logan
30th Virginia • 45th Virginia • 50th Virginia • 51st Virginia Battalion Sharpshooters

Patton's Brigade Col. George S. Patton (mw)[12] Capt. Edmund S. Read, Lt. Col. John C. McDonald
22nd Virginia • 23rd Virginia Battalion • 26th Virginia Reserves

Smith's Brigade Col. Thomas Smith
36th Virginia • 60th Virginia • 45th Virginia Battalion • Thomas Legion

Kershaw's Division Maj. Gen. Joseph B. Kershaw
Kershaw's Brigade Col. John W. Henagan (c)[13] Brig. Gen. James Conner (w)[14,] Maj. James M. Goggin
*2nd South Carolina • 3rd South Carolina • 7th South Carolina • 8th South Carolina • 15th South Carolina
20th South Carolina • 3rd South Carolina Battalion*

Humphrey's Brigade Brig. Gen. Benjamin G. Humphreys
13th Mississippi • 17th Mississippi • 18th Mississippi • 21st Mississippi

Wofford's Brigade Brig. Gen. William T. Wofford
*16th Georgia • 18th Georgia • 24th Georgia • 3rd Georgia Battalion • Cobb's (Georgia) Legion
Phillips (Georgia) Legion*

Bryan's Brigade Brig. Gen. Goode Bryan[15], Col. James P. Simms
10th Georgia • 50th Georgia • 51st Georgia • 53rd Georgia

Cavalry Maj. Gen. Fitzhugh Lee (w)[16]
Lomax's Division Maj. Gen. Lunsford L. Lomax
Imboden's Brigade Brig. Gen. John Imboden[17], Col. George Smith
18th Virginia • 23rd Virginia • 62nd Virginia Mounted Infantry

Johnson's Brigade Brig. Gen. Bradley T. Johnson
8th Virginia • 21st Virginia • 22nd Virginia • 34th Virginia • 36th Virginia

McCausland's Brigade Brig. Gen. John M. McClausland
14th Virginia • 16th Virginia • 17th Virginia • 25th Virginia • 37th Virginia Battalion

Jackson's Brigade Brig. Gen. William L. Jackson, Brig. Gen. Henry B. Davidson,
Lt. Col. William Thompson[18]
2nd Maryland • 19th Virginia • 20th Virginia • 46th Virginia Battalion • 47th Virginia Battalion

Lee's Division Maj. Gen. Fitzhugh Lee (w)[19], Brig. Gen. Williams C. Wickham[20],
Brig. Gen. Thomas L. Rosser
Wickham's Brigade Brig. Gen. Williams C. Wickham, Col. Thomas T. Munford
1st Virginia • 2nd Virginia • 3rd Virginia • 4th Virginia

Rosser's Brigade Brig. Gen. Thomas L. Rosser, Lt. Col. Richard H. Dulany,
Col. Oliver R. Funston, Jr.
7th Virginia • 11th Virginia • 12th Virginia • 35th Virginia Battalion

Payne's Brigade Col. William H. Payne
5th Virginia • 6th Virginia • 15th Virginia

Artillery Brig. Gen. Armistead L. Long[21], Col. Thomas H. Carter
Braxton's Battalion Lt. Col. Carter M. Braxton
Carpenter's Alleghany (Virginia) Battery • Hardwicke's Lee (Virginia) Battery • Cooper's Stafford (Virginia) Battery

Nelson's Battalion Lt. Col. William Nelson
Kirkpatrick's (Virginia) Amherst Battery • Massie's (Virginia) Battery, Milledge, Jr.'s (Georgia) Regular Battery

King's Battalion Lt. Col. J. Floyd King, Maj. William McLaughlin
Bryan's (Virginia) Lewisburg Battery • Chapman's (Virginia) Monroe Battery
Lowry's (Virginia) Wise Legion Battery

Cutshaw's Battalion Maj. Wilfred E. Cutshaw
Carrington's (Virginia) Charlottesville Battery • Tanner's (Virginia) Richmond Courtney Battery
Garber's (Virginia) Staunton Battery

Breathed's Horse Artillery Battalion Maj. James Breathed
Griffin's 2nd (Maryland) Battery • Johnston's (Virginia) Charlottesville Battery • Thomson's (Virginia) Ashby
Battery • 1st Stuart Horse Battery • Jackson's (Virginia) Charlottesville Battery • Shoemaker's (Virginia)
Lynchburg Battery • Lurty's (Virginia) Roanoke Battery • McClannahan's (Virginia) Staunton Battery

* * *

(cm)

1 *Killed at Third Winchester*

2 *Succeeded to command Rodes' division after Third Winchester. Mortally wounded at Cedar Creek on October 19, 1864, and died the next day.*

3 *Severely wounded at Cedar Creek and did not return to active service before the war ended*

4 *See note #2*

5 *Wounded at Third Winchester*

6 *Killed at Third Winchester*

7 *Directed Second Corps while Early was in command of the army*

8 *Captured at Fisher's Hill*

9 *Consisted of the remnants of 14 regiments from the "Stonewall" Division which was decimated at the Battle of Spotsylvania Court House on May 12, 1864*

10 *Severely wounded at Third Winchester and incapacitated for further active service; York's Brigade contained regiments of two former Louisiana Brigades*

11 *Wounded at Third Winchester*

12 *Mortally Wounded at Third Winchester*

13 *Captured at Third Winchester and imprisoned at Johnson's Island, Ohio, where he died on April 26, 1865*

14 *Severely wounded, lost a leg to amputation at Hupp's Hill*

15 *Resigned from his command on September 20, 1864, because of chronic ill health and returned to Georgia*

16 *Wounded at Third Winchester*

17 *Suffered a severe case of typhoid fever in the fall of 1864 that incapacitated him from further field command and he would be transferred to command a prisoner-of-war camp in the Deep South*

18 *Commanded brigade at Tom's Brook*

19 *Wounded at Third Winchester*

20 *Resigned from army and took his seat in the Confederate Congress on October 5, 1864*

21 *Absent from the army during the campaign due to illness*

Suggested Reading

THE SHENANDOAH VALLEY CAMPAIGN
OF 1864

The Shenandoah Valley Campaign of 1864
Gary W. Gallagher, editor
The University of North Carolina Press 2006
ISBN-13: 978-0-8078-3005-5

Gallagher's book collects essays from some of the leading experts on the campaign: William Bergen, Keith Bohannon, Andre Fleche, Joseph T. Glatthaar, Robert K. Krick, Robert E. L. Krick, William J. Miller, Aaron Sheehan-Dean, William G. Thomas, Joan Waugh, and Gallagher himself. This excellent collection of essays includes topics relating to the battles of Fisher's Hill, Tom's Brook, and Cedar Creek; the Union high command during the campaign; Horatio Wright; Valley civilians; and much more.

For more on Gallagher's work examining Jubal Early's postwar impact on Lost Cause memory (as discussed in Appendix C), see "Jubal A. Early, the Lost Cause, and Civil War History" in *The Myth of the Lost Cause and Civil War History* (Indiana University Press, 2000).

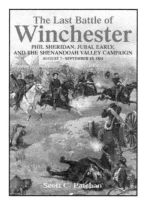

The Last Battle of Winchester: Phil Sheridan, Jubal Early and the Shenandoah Valley Campaign August 7-September 19, 1864
Scott C. Patchan
Savas Beatie 2013
ISBN: 1932714987

Historically, Cedar Creek has been considered the pivotal battle of the campaign. After years of exhaustive research, Scott Patchan contends that the critical battle was actually at Third Winchester. *The Last Battle of Winchester* is a must-read book for anyone who wants a full understanding of the battle and its inner workings.

Shenandoah Summer: The 1864 Valley Campaign
Scott C. Patchan
Bison Books 2009
ISBN-13: 978-0803218864

Patchan's study of the summer campaign—between the raid on Washington and the autumn campaign of 1864—is an exhaustive microstudy of a very important political and military campaign that was overshadowed by what happened after. Using a plethora of primary sources, he reconstructs these oft-forgotten battles that set the stage for the most pivotal campaign in the Shenandoah Valley.

From Winchester to Cedar Creek: The Shenandoah Campaign of 1864
Jeffry Wert
South Mountain Press 1987
Reprinted in paperback by
    Touchstone/Simon and Schuster 1989
Stackpole Books 1997
ISBN: 0-8117-0672-9

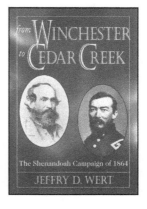

In *From Winchester to Cedar Creek*, Jeffry Wert examines the entire 1864 campaign. His analysis ranges from the individual battles to the campaign's impact on the Eastern Theater and the Union war effort itself. Utilizing primary materials, Wert weaves a highly detailed yet easy-to-read micro tactical study.

About the Authors

Daniel T. Davis is a graduate of Longwood University with a degree in Public History. He has worked as a seasonal historian at Fredericksburg and Spotsylvania National Military Park and a living history interpreter at Appomattox Court House National Historic Site. Dan is the author or co-author of numerous books in the Emerging Civil War Series as well as articles in Blue and Gray Magazine, Hallowed Ground and Civil War Times. He is the senior education manager with the American Battlefield Trust.

Phillip S. Greenwalt hold as B.A. in History from Wheeling Jesuit University and a M.A. in American History from George Mason University. He has worked for the National Park Service for more than 15 years at various parks, including George Washington Birthplace National Monument, Everglades National Park, Fredericksburg and Spotsylvania National Military Park, and Morristown National Historical Park. He currently resides in Frederick, Maryland.

Daniel and Phill are both contributors to the blog Emerging Civil War, www.emergingcivilwar.com.

EMERGING CIVIL WAR SERIES